BROTHERS
OF THE ZODIAC

EARTH

MAXWELL THOMAS

Cover design © 2018 by Niki Lenhart
nikilen-designs.com

Published by Zarra Knightley Publishing
zarraknightleypublishing.com

ISBN 978-1-946907-21-9 (Trade Paperback)

10 9 8 7 6 5 4 3 2 1

FIRST EDITION

PROLOGUE

TROY
1183 BC

I

THE BEAUTIFUL DARK-SKINNED WOMAN glided among the dead on the plain before the city of Troy. Ten-feet tall, she wore a gown of gold, its hem swinging through the blood, mud, and gore of the field. The angry calls of the crows contrasted sharply with the gentle tinkle of the golden tips of her hair as they moved together. She looked side to side, from body to body, studying their souls.

Hermes had not yet come to take them to Hades; she knew she didn't have very long. Her own six-man army fought in the city of Troy. Cancer, Scorpio, Taurus, and Sagittarius fought for the Greeks; Leo and Aries defended Troy.

The Greeks would take the city and sack it. Her six men would survive. But, for her name to survive, she needed more warriors. For the human race to survive, she needed more men to worship, remember, and assist her.

In return, she would bless them with the power of the elements. Earth, Air, Fire, and Water were under her command, and she would happily separate them among the men, giving them power beyond other mortals. For here, in Troy, Zeus planned to destroy all of his sons and daughters, to begin the human race anew — without the heroes and demigods of old.

She bent and effortlessly plucked a man by the backplate of his armor, lifting him from the blood-soaked mud. He took a breath, then threw up blood as she held him in the air.

"You are my warrior, named *Gal.Gal.*" She set him on his feet in the place he had once lay.

His wound was apparent, a hole in his breastplate just above the heart. He looked down, then back up at the woman, but she moved on. She had to hurry.

"Wait! Who are you? Athene?"

"Nay," she said, and bent to help another man up. "Arise, my warrior. You are named *Absin.*"

This second fighter — a hoplite Greek by his armor — turned to look at the man who followed the woman. "Is this Hades?"

"No," he said. "Who is she?"

"I don't know," the man said. "Who are you?"

"Come," the woman said. She tapped another hoplite.

He opened his eyes that had been closed in eternal sleep. "Lady Hera?"

"Nay," the woman said, sounding more and more frustrated. "You are my warrior, *Gula.* Come. Follow me."

She chose three more confused men, naming them each Suhurmas, Kun, and Giserin. All six followed her to the western side of Troy, where they could hear the shouts of victory. All six were equally mixed of Trojans and Greeks. All six knew they had been dead.

She looked out into the distance and could see Hermes gathering souls to him, ready to bring them to the Elysian

Fields or the Asphodel Meadows. His shining countenance, and his golden caduceus, summoned the souls up from the bodies, into his arms.

"You are my warriors. I am the goddess Ishtar."

The men looked at each other in total confusion.

"I am older than Ares and Athene. I am older than Zeus. I am older than Chronos. I am of the beginning and the Void."

One man bowed down. The other five looked among each other, thinking about it, before they did as well.

"I give you power, strength, and immortality — until you find the one you love in another man's eyes. And then, I shall set your eyes among the stars, so your souls shall live forever."

"What is our purpose, Great Ishtar?" asked the man who had bowed down first.

"Gal.Gal, you live and exist to assist the mortals. To help them grow and inspire them. To aid them and assist them. And to keep my name." She glanced up at the walls. "Your comrades will find you. They will teach you."

"This is crazy." said a man, his face buried in the dirt.

No lightning bolts came down from the sky to destroy him for his blasphemy. No arrows from Apollo rained down. The sun did not grow dark. In fact, when they lifted their faces from the dirt, the woman had disappeared.

"What just happened?" asked the man called Kun.

The six men rose to their feet. "Gal.Gal," said Suhurmas. "What kind of name is that?"

"I can't even pronounce yours," said Gal.Gal.

"It means Goat-Fish," said Gula. "Capricorn."

"You look like a Goat-Fish," said the hoplite called Absin.

"You look like your mother's ass," said Capricorn.

Absin started after Capricorn, but two men held him back. Gal.Gal held back Capricorn, who merely leered at Absin.

"Stop fighting," said Kun, standing aside. "We're in this together. We're warriors of a Goddess."

Gal.Gal pointed out at the field. "Do you want to be one of them?" Hermes still did his work. They could see him. "Do you want to spend eternity pining for your wife and children? At least we can go back. At least we can live among men again."

"And guide them like gods," said Capricorn.

"That's not what we're here for," Kun said.

Finally, Giserin said quietly, "Let's find our comrades, like she said. Maybe they can help us."

2

For the third time, the man named Gal.Gal — who found out his Greek name was Gemini — got stabbed in the back.

"We have to get you out of that armor," said Kun, who in Greek was called Pisces. "Anybody who's Trojan is going to be attacked."

Absin — in Greek, named Virgo — dragged a body into a house and stripped it. "Here. This should fit you."

Libra, who had been named Giserin by the Goddess, also changed into Greek hoplite armor. When he came out of the alleyway he had changed in, the other five men were gathered together in a knot, facing another group of five men directly across from them. Between them, men ran after women and children. Men ran past them, carrying bulging bags of loot. Another man killed a Trojan who didn't even wear armor, right in front of them.

"I think we found our comrades," said Libra.

"Or they found us," said Pisces.

Then the six men walked across the road. Herded in the center of the group of six were two men in Trojan armor. The new group met them in the middle of the road.

They looked each other up and down.

"Hail, brother," said Gemini.

A man stepped forward, his arm outstretched. "Hail, brother. I am Sagittarius."

Gemini clasped Sagittarius' forearm and Sagittarius pulled him into an embrace.

A large man rolled his eyes. "By the Gods. Here?"

"Let's go," said the Trojan in the center. "Let us walk together."

They left the great city to the Greeks and their Gods.

3

"The Bull of Heaven?"

The large man crossed his arms and regarded the new Trojan. "Scales of Justice?"

"I wasn't insulting you," said Libra, who drank the wine left at the shore by the Greeks. The Greeks had been in this camp for far too long, and now that they had the city, no one was in camp except the twelve men of Ishtar, scattered throughout the tents and campfires.

"I don't understand. What were we doing wrong?"

"She didn't mention that you did anything wrong. You still can't die, because you survived the war."

"Maybe six of us aren't enough," said Aries,
Libra only shrugged.

"Besides, why else would we all be here in Troy?" Aries waved his hand toward the sea at their backs. "All the gods, sons of gods, and us."

"Are you originally Greek?" asked Libra.

Aries shook his head. "North."

The man called Scorpio ran into the tent. "The Virgin disappeared!"

"What do you mean?" asked Taurus.

"I was talking to him, and he faded away, right in front of me. I tried to catch him, but my hands went through him."

The three men looked between each other. "Find the rest," ordered Aries.

As they searched, Cancer came upon Capricorn. Capricorn followed Cancer to the tent, but when Cancer got to the tent, Capricorn had disappeared, fading away silently.

Seven remained by the time they got together. Sitting at a campfire, all of the men watched as Aries stood up. "I feel —" then his voice went silent, even though he still spoke, because his lips were moving.

The men could see through him to the tent beyond. Aries looked up at the men, a confused look on his face. Then, he faded away.

"Gods ..." whispered Taurus.

"Maybe if we hold onto each other," said Gemini, reaching for the person next to him. But Libra started fading away.

Gemini kept reaching for people, finally joining hands with the first of the old veterans, Sagittarius. Sagittarius held tightly onto Gemini's hand. Gemini embraced Sagittarius.

Neither disappeared from each other or the shores of Troy.

CAPRICORN

THE WESTERN FRONTIER
MARCH 8, 1869

I

WHEN ISHTAR CLAIMED ME FROM THE UNDERWORLD, I wanted to be king. Frederick was king of Austria, Richard of England, Phillip of France, and Henry of the Holy Roman Empire. Saladin had captured Jerusalem.

Instead, I was a knight of the French army, and later of the English army. I strove through the ranks to general, though it took me twenty years.

Sometimes, it was noticed that I hadn't aged. Sometimes, I had to drop everything and move to a different country, taking a different name, learning a different language and way of life.

For years, I would begin at the lowest rungs of the military ladders and have to climb my way upward; sometimes I did this in less than a year. Other times it took much longer.

But here, in America, no one noticed.

Money can do amazing things here.

We were somewhere in the middle of the Missouri territory. The locomotive pulling my car, and the five cars behind me full of provisions and bunkhouses for the workers, inched its way westward. We would make it to the Utah territory first.

Although I didn't own Union Pacific, I planned to soon. Once I would get to Promontory, Utah, I would make it my goal to own the railroad that I built. All I had to do was get rid of Durant. Because he had screwed so many people, he was not long for this world, I would make sure of it.

"General?" A Negro boy peeked his head into my car.

I sighed as I looked away from the window, where I had been watching the workers. "I thought I said I didn't want to be disturbed."

"Supervisor says it's an emergency."

"Which one?" I got up from my chair, pulled down my vest and checked my gold watch.

"Daisy."

I snorted. "He thinks anything amiss is an emergency. Fine, I'll see him."

"He wants you to come to him, sir."

"Hell."

I grabbed my jacket from the coatrack and followed the boy out the door. As I followed him, people stopped what they were doing and either bowed or nodded to me. They knew who I was.

The tents were up already. We were going to be a few days in this part of Missouri territory, so the merchants and prostitutes would be setting up to separate the men from their money. I saw the sign for the wine and spirits. *Figures that would be the first one up.*

The boy dragged me to the front of the line, past the workers, to a crowd of about ten men gathered in a circle, looking down at something on the ground. One of the men noticed me, hit another man, and they all slowly turned to face me. Then they stepped aside.

Four men's bodies lay in a lump on the ground. One of them had an arrow sticking out of his back.

"So, what's this?" I asked.

Daisy was pale. He probably had lost his lunch over this. He was a small, thin man, effeminate. I dressed him in women's clothes and called him Daisy. The name had stuck, but he had a whip in his hand, so no one called him that to his face — unless they wanted to lose an eye.

"Apaches dropped them off," said Caleb, another supervisor. "They're advance scouts."

"So bury 'em," I said. "What do you need me for?"

Caleb held out a paper. I unfolded it. In large block letters were the words: "GO HOME".

"Damn injuns."

I spat on the ground, crumpling up the paper. This was the first group of advance scouts that had been returned with a message. The first two sets were discovered by other scouts, dead. They'd been buried where they were found. We'd passed them a couple of days ago.

"Get the priest and bury them," I said.

I turned from the group and walked back, wondering what it would be like to fuck an Indian.

2

I hated Sundays. No work got done in the morning, thanks to the damn priests who traveled with us. They talked the last Chief Engineer into having Sunday mornings and holidays off, like Good Friday and Christmas. It was a waste of time for me. The engine would sit until afternoon, and then the men would come back all purified and full of grace, ready to work like dogs.

Except for the one who shared my bed that morning.

Caleb absently rubbed my chest hair as my arm was tucked beneath him, his head on my shoulder. Caleb's dark skin glistened in the heat of the bed.

"About the scouts ..." he began.

"What about them?"

"Nobody wants to go out anymore."

"What do they want, hazard pay?" I grunted and sat up.

I grabbed a towel from the washbasin beside the bed and wiped him off my abdomen.

"They don't want to deal with the Indians," he said, his head on his hand, elbow crooked on the bed as he lay on his side, looking at me. "*I* don't want to deal with the Indians."

"You said they were Apaches?"

"I guess?"

"This is Minnesota. There's no Apaches in Minnesota."

Caleb shrugged. I threw his pants at him.

He knew what that meant. He put them on, and reached for his shirt at the foot of the bed. I pulled on my breeches and buttoned them up.

He was out the door in three minutes flat.

I sat shirtless and barefoot in the heat; all the windows were open in the car. I had my back to the door of the car. I was trying to decide what to do next, when the door opened and a hot desert breeze blew in. It rustled the papers on my desk, throwing them haphazardly into the air. I whirled around to give a good tongue-lashing to the son of a bitch who came in.

A woman stepped in. She wore a red skirt, flowing, wide, and in layers down to her bare feet. Her bare arms and bare chest were perfectly formed. On her head sat a crown with two golden snakes coming out of the side of her head like horns. The ends of her long curly black hair ended in gold and blue metal tips and tinkled as she moved her head. Her face was darker-skinned, from the desert. She held what could have been a torch in one hand, a thick bundle of sticks. Her green and gold crystal wings brushed the doorway as she entered. The door closed behind her.

I had seen her once, a long, long time ago, when she fetched me from the Underworld, the land of Ereshkigal. I had not seen her since.

"Oh, my Lady Ishtar," I whispered, and dropped to my knees before her, bowing my head.

"*Suhur.Mas,*" she said, her voice like a beautiful songbird that reached into my bones. I prostrated myself before her, my fingertips brushing the hem of her dress, my forehead on the wooden floor of the railroad car.

"I am disappointed in you."

Oh, no, I thought, knowing she knew my thoughts.

"My Lady," I said, "I have given aid and comfort to your children. I have given money to your causes."

"Yet you hurt the land I have entrusted to you."

I burrowed my head down, "This train will bring people to the land, so —"

"It is not the train," she said. "You make sand of mountains."

The dynamite. We did have to use it a few times to blow through some mountains, even though I could have parted the mountain myself. But if I did that, then I would have been run out on a rail for being a freak.

"My Lady, I —"

15

"You will choose your mate and your heir within one season."

If I chose a mate, then I would be mortal and die. But choosing an heir?

She stepped back away from me and aimed the bundle of sticks at my head. "Do you disagree?"

She'd kill me. Right then and there, she'd kill me. What was I going to say? I know my mind whirled, thinking of who in this mess of men would be my mate, and who, out of all of them, could be my heir.

The wind blew again, and I dared to look up. She was gone.

God, I needed a drink.

3

Sunday night and Helltown was in full swing.

I was already feeling mellow. The visit by the Lady Ishtar, the great Goddess of the Sumerians, made me drink half of my supply of rum and I was looking to refill my stock. I made lists of men to choose as mates, and none of the ones I knew at the moment were up to my standards. Not a one. I didn't even want to think about heirs.

I had a season, until the full-fledged springtime, to find them.

"Mr. Casement, how pleasant to see you!" said a man from the outside of Yates' Wine and Spirits tent.

I looked Yates over. He was of better genteel stock than the men I'd listed, but he was pot-bellied and always smelled of onions.

No, not him.

"Good to see you, Mr. Yates. What do you have for rum?"

"I'm sure I can find something for you."

Someone bumped into me, someone soft and smelling of rosewater.

"Penny," I said, turning around as a woman slipped her hands around my waist.

"Missus Martin, if you please," she said, giggling.

"Missus? You married since two weeks ago?"

"I'm a Missus since I got three girls of my own."

Yates's mouth dropped open. "Ohhhh, there will be a catfight here for certain!"

"I'm not getting involved," I said.

"We just picked up some Rebel boys," Penny whispered in my ear.

She knew I liked men with a Southern twang as opposed to my New York accent. They could read the Bible and I would enjoy that almost as much as having sex with them.

She stepped back. "They're down yonder."

"Hold that rum for me, Mr. Yates. I'll come back for it."

"Indeed, Mr. Casement."

Penny tucked her arm in mine and guided me toward the thicker part of Helltown. In here were casinos, more wine and spirits. Among them sat tents for prostitution nestled in with churches, opium dens and preachers. Campfires burned to the side while men gathered around singing, laughing, playing with women, or what could have been boys, sitting on their laps.

Whites stayed away from blacks, and Rebels usually stayed away from Yankees. The war had only ended four years ago, but there were still bad feelings on both sides.

Fights sometimes broke out in the bunkhouses on the train, which were set up usually for whites.

Penny pulled me toward a campfire, where a man sat sharpening a Bowie knife. She smiled at the man.

"What happened to your friends?" she asked.

The man shrugged. He was white, with shining blue eyes and blond hair that came to his shoulders. He wore a beat-up Confederate officer's hat that he probably never took off. He wore a coat buttoned up tight in the cold, flannel pants, and worn boots.

"They went over to one of the tents. Couldn't stand the weather and the girls were getting cold."

Penny stepped aside for me. "This is General Jack Casement. He's our Chief Engineer."

"General?" asked the man, giving me the side-eye.

"Union."

"I see." He stood up. "Lieutenant Colonel Casey Donovan."

"Greyback," I said.

"Got any problem with that?"

"Not at all. As long as you work."

"I work." He shrugged again. "Nothing else to do."

"Where you from?"

"Virginia. My plantation got taken over by the Yankees."

"Then do you have a problem with being under a Union boss?"

"You won. Congratulations." What he probably wanted to say was, *"I hope you choke on it."*

I nodded my head up toward the railroad car. "You sound like you'll do. Come with me."

"Do? Do for what?"

But I started walking up the hill. I turned around to see if he was going to follow me, but he didn't. Penny was talking to him. He looked angry. He sheathed the big knife in his boot and stormed toward me.

This was going to be interesting.

4

I opened the door to the car to let him in first. It was much warmer than it was outside.

Like a gentleman of good breeding, he removed his hat when he stepped inside.

"So this is what we're working for," he said. "To keep you comfortable."

"You were the plantation master," I said. "You know how it is."

"I never said I was the owner."

He took off his jacket. He was too well-built to be a plantation master. A supervisor, maybe. Besides, most of the plantation masters were never in the Confederate army.

"I said my plantation got taken over."

"You'll have to tell me your story, Colonel," I said, as I poured him a snifter of brandy.

He looked at the drink, then at me. "I don't drink."

"Even though it'll warm up your insides?" I took the snifter and poured it back in the bottle. Waste not.

"I used to drink. It made me an idiot."

"That's one of the things it's supposed to do. Or make you happy."

He took a seat across from where I stood. "It never made me happy."

"There's a story there, too." I sat down in the chair next to him.

"What makes you so interested in me and my story?"

"A few things. How did you come here?"

"Looking for work like everybody else."

"If you stayed in Virginia, you'd find plenty of work there."

"Got bored with Virginia."

"Mmmhmm," I said, looking him over. "Why don't you get more comfortable? You should be warm in all those layers."

"Don't want to get too comfortable. I'm going back out there."

"You don't have to."

He gazed at me. "What's that supposed to mean?"

"You can stay in here for tonight."

He looked around. There were no couches in the car, and my bed was blocked off by a curtain. What went through his mind was the same thing that went through so many other men's minds. I could see the different emotions and thoughts play on his face: confusion, then a slow realization. What would follow? Disgust or acceptance?

I didn't get to find out because the door to my car opened and Daisy walked in like he owned the place. He saw me sitting in the chair, and then saw Casey sitting opposite me. Daisy normally entertained me on Sunday nights, but tonight I wasn't in the mood for him.

Daisy stalked forward, advancing on Casey. This was a side of Daisy I hadn't seen in a long time. Someone was taking his place on Sunday night, and he could not abide it. I expected Casey to fight with Daisy. The thought made me swell in my breeches.

Instead, Casey rose. "I see you have company," he said, and plucked his jacket and hat from the coat rack. I half-rose, disappointed, but he was out the door before I could get a word out.

I glared at Daisy. Daisy preened like a peacock, having won the contest. I stormed up to him and punched him hard in the face. He fell down. He put his hands to cover his head as I kicked him in the ribs.

"You spoiled little snot, get out!"

I picked him up by the back of his collar and half-dragged him to the door. I threw open the door and tossed him out, head-first, into the frozen ground. Then I slammed the door after him.

Casey was probably already down the hill, so I'd lost my chance. I passed my hand through my hair, slicking it back. There was always tomorrow.

5

Helltown was three miles from the new bridge being built. The goal was to have the bridge finished by the time we got there. Helltown packed up that morning to get ready to be closer to the bridge that night. We would have ties laid down enough track in a couple of days leading to the bridge.

On the other side of the bridge we were laying track, because I, for one, did not want the train to stay on the bridge for long. I knew there were Mormons working on the bridge. They were well-known for their carpentry skills, but the weight of the train on the bridge for too long made me nervous. Keep me on *terra firma*, where I had more control.

I took a breath outside, mostly to look over the livestock of men working, to decide who to pick for my liaison for the evening. Really, though, I was looking for Casey.

While I was outside, a man rode up to the locomotive. He stopped when he saw me.

"Do you know where the Chief Engineer is?"

"That would be me. Jack Casement."

"I'm from the North Bridge."

He was dressed simply. Probably a Mormon. *Too bad; he was cute.*

"What can I do for you?" I asked.

"The bridge isn't ready."

I rocked back. "What?"

"We've still got—"

"You started before we even got to Utah territory, and you mean to tell me the bridge isn't ready yet? What the hell have you been doing?"

"We lost some men to the Indians."

"What Indians?"

He shrugged. "They attacked our camp one night. Killed fifteen men."

"Fifteen out of a hundred?"

"Less than that."

"Since when? I was told there were over a hundred workers."

"Not since winter set in."

"Goddammit." He winced when I swore. "How many men do you need?"

"Fifty or so?"

"Fifty or so. Like I can spare that many."

The men laying the beds would have to go work on the bridge. That meant that the men laying the track would have to dig for the beds as well. I would have a mutiny on my hands within days. Digging the beds was harder work than laying the track, and bedwork was left mostly to the Negroes.

"You can have twenty men." I would get Daisy and his crew to go with this Mormon back to the bridge. "How much is left?"

"Sixty yards."

"To be built or laid?"

"Laid."

That meant the bridge itself was built, it was the track that needed to go in, which was the most dangerous part of the work because they had to work on the thin bridge itself. One wrong step and the person fell over the side into the icy river.

I stepped out from behind the locomotive. "Mitch!" That was Daisy's real name.

He came running over to me like a good dog.

"Go with this man to the North Bridge and take twenty men with you. Better bring tools, just in case."

"Yes, sir," Daisy said, and looked up at the Mormon, who turned his horse to follow Daisy.

The man pranced away without even a thank-you. I should lame his horse and make him walk.

I sent Caleb to fetch a new group of men from the bunkhouse. They would have to start a day earlier than usual. Most of them were probably hung over, but I really didn't care. The work had to get done.

6

The boom from the dynamite echoed through the valley. Mountains into sand. Hills into flatland. That's what we did.

We were within sight of the bridge. The ground was frozen and needed to be softened up. We had plenty of dynamite now that the war was over. I got a telegraph from the last station a few miles back. We were to meet in Utah, and the Chief Engineer who got to Promontory Summit first would get an extra $1000. That was going to be me.

I'd already sent a crew across the bridge to start building the bed so that the locomotive, the heaviest part of the train, would not be sitting on the bridge for long. My car was after the coal car, and I didn't want to sit on the bridge at all.

I went out and drove the men faster, mostly the supervisors, with promises of more money or food or whatever it took. What they really wanted was rest, and I wasn't going to give them that. Sunday mornings was all I would give in and, even then, it was grudgingly.

On Saturday night, I went out looking for Casey. I wanted him to share my bed in the evening and Sunday morning. Because he had shown no emotion when Daisy showed up, I thought that maybe — just maybe — he would enjoy an evening with me.

I found him in the bunkhouse. The men already knew about me, about my taste in men, and some of them gave me the side-eye when I walked by. I asked men about him, and they seemed to know him. He had been promoted to a supervisor of a crew already.

"Donovan," I said, as I approached his bunk. He lay there, staring up at the bunk above him. He was smoking a cigarette — a habit I never cared for.

He sat up and swung his long legs out of the bunk, then got to his feet. "Mr. Casement. What brings you here?"

"I'm looking for you, actually. We never finished out conversation from last week."

"Uh huh."

The men around us were staring at us. They knew. I assumed Casey knew. He looked away from me, gathered his coat. He must have known. Under all my layers of clothes, my cock gave a little twitch.

I led the way out. I didn't bother to look behind me to see if the man followed; I knew he was going to.

When I got to my car, he was a couple of steps behind, his coat bundled around him. He said, "Something I have to ask."

"What's that?"

"You got a bathtub?"

I laughed. "A bathtub? What for?"

"What else do you use a bathtub for?"

"No, I don't."

I held the door open for him. He looked at me, looked at the door. He looked back at me again. He turned around and walked away from me.

I stood there, dumbstruck. That had never happened to me before. Never! Nobody ever walked away from me.

I slammed shut the door and glared at his retreating back. I lost sight of him when he ducked between two cars. How dare he! Because I didn't have a bathtub? What did that have to do with anything?

"Son of a bitch!" I threw open the door to my car and stormed inside.

Nobody showed up that night, so I drank myself into oblivion and slept alone.

7

In all my years alive after Ishtar claimed me, I never had a hangover. I had forgotten how they could incapacitate one — especially after the dynamite started in the afternoon.

Also, I couldn't get drunk. What had happened to me? Did Lady Ishtar already take my immortality? Had I found my mate? Or my heir?

I couldn't think with the thunderous booming outside and in my head. I forced myself to sit at my desk, though I was only in my long johns and barefoot.

Then the train started moving. I wasn't ready for it, and threw up all over the mahogany desk and the papers scattered there.

Normally I got my sea legs quickly after the train started moving, but I didn't dare move from the mess that dripped onto the carpet. I threw up again and again until nothing was left and I was only heaving.

I stumbled out of the mess near my desk and dropped into a chair nearby. I didn't look out the windows, and I didn't stand up, not thinking that I could.

The train eventually stopped, having run its few yards. I risked getting out of the chair and went to the window.

We were on the goddamn bridge.

No one would be able to get to my car because the locomotive and the car took up the width of the bridge. How long were we going to be here?

I went to the rear door that led to a small platform between my car and the freight car behind me. I opened the door and got a blast of fresh cold air that woke me up and took away the stench of the vomit. I glanced over the side of the platform and thought I was going to faint.

It was straight down ... into the river.

I lurched back into the car and stood against the closed door. The train started moving again. I held onto the wall and shambled like a drunken man to the nearest chair. Holding onto the armrests, I took deep breaths as the train clacked along the new tracks of the bridge.

Would it hold all our weight?

The car swayed as we chugged along the bridge, not moving fast enough, in my opinion. We were suspended in the air, at the mercy of the winds, something I never liked because of the lack of solid ground beneath my feet. Solid ground was where my power came from.

I had a fleeting thought: *I hoped that man would never learn to fly.*

Then I felt the bump as we crossed from the bridge onto land. I got up and walked to the door of the car, throwing it open again. We were moving slowly enough so I could jump off. I know I looked like hell, but I wanted the earth beneath me. My feet froze in the snow-covered bed, but at least it was ground.

My Negro boy came running up and took one look at me. I know he saw what a wreck I looked like. I barked orders at him to go clean my car. I stood and watched the cars slowly go by before I started walking back to my car. My feet grew cold, but my head was clearer now.

I would have to get a bathtub.

8

Brigham Young looked ready to split rails. He was short, but rustically built, with the beginnings of a wiseman's beard. His men were just as built, ready for pioneering and hard work.

They were, after all, heretics.

They had been chased from one end of the country to the other because of their beliefs. I personally didn't care about their religion or how they practiced it. All I cared about was whether or not they would work.

They would work on Sunday mornings, but not on Saturdays. I accepted that. The days were getting longer as we approached Promontory Summit, and my days were being numbered because of Lady Ishtar's demands. I had fought off a cold — maybe even the flu — something I hadn't had in a long time. I was just beginning to feel better when Young arrived with his men.

Helltown moved with us, and the Mormons didn't dare go there. That worked out fine for me. They were hard workers, and they were being paid well. I never saw a female Mormon. I wondered if they even existed.

Casey Donovan moved up in the ranks to be a supervisor. I kept my eye on him. As the time went by, I thought a lot about him, and chose to make him my mate. As for an heir ... maybe I should leave that to Lady Ishtar.

It wasn't until April when I felt good enough to go through Helltown to try and find Donovan. We were within sight of Promontory Summit and would be the first ones there. I'd get my $1,000 and die a happy man.

I found Donovan outside of a brothel. He smoked a cigarette and sat alone.

"No girls?" I asked him.

"Don't trust 'em. They'll steal my money and give me syphilis."

"You know ..." I got closer to him. "I got a bathtub."

"I heard about you, Mr. Casement." He exhaled smoke through his nose.

"What have you heard?"

"That you prefer boys."

"Not always. I enjoy the company of men as well."

He looked me over. Then he stood up, and stomped out the cigarette. His boots were worn, held together by ropes tied around the sole and toe.

"Why don't you buy some new boots?" I asked him.

"Helltown doesn't sell boots."

"I might have an extra pair."

"You're smaller than me," he said.

"We'll just have to see about that." I grinned at him.

He chuckled, knowing what I was alluding to. Foot size and dick size should be the same. If that were true, this man's cock was probably up to the middle of his stomach.

He followed me to the car. I opened the door and let him in first. Then I went to the servant's quarters and shook awake a young Negro servant.

"Get me hot water."

After rubbing sleep out of his eyes, the boy jumped up to do my bidding. I didn't care where he got the hot water, as long as he showed up with it in the next ten minutes.

I walked into the car. Donovan was standing in the middle of it, not sure whether to sit down on the fine velvet chairs. He knew he was out of place in this fancy railroad car of mine. He looked even more threadbare than he had before. Some of his clothes were probably the same ones as when I first met him.

"You can get comfortable," I said. "I have someone getting the hot water."

I walked over to a curtain and pulled it open. On the other side was a rather small wooden tub, big enough to sit in with your knees up but not stretch out in. I got it from a cooper who made barrels for wine.

He took off his jacket first. Then a flannel shirt beneath. Beneath that was another grey cotton button-down shirt with fancy silver buttons — his uniform from the war.

Under that was a tattered and yellowed long-sleeved shirt. Under *that* was a frayed and yellow cotton shirt, the under shirt, that fell apart in his hands.

Beneath that was his skin — his white skin. He had very light hair on his chest and under his arms. His chest was firm and strong, his abdomen perfectly formed into six hard blocks.

He stunk to high heaven. I couldn't help but grimace at the stench.

"Sorry," he said as his red blush came up from his chest to his cheeks.

"I must get something for you to wear. You are not putting on those clothes again."

He glanced at the pile of shirts on the floor. He bent and picked out his grey uniform shirt. "Not this."

"I'll have it washed. If it stays together."

I took it from him and held it an arm's length away from me, wrinkling my nose. Knowing how tough soldiers' clothes could be, it just might survive.

The knock on the door drew my attention. I opened it and the Negro boy stood there with a bucket. It wouldn't be enough, but it would be a good start. I took the bucket from him, careful not to slop it around on the carpet of the railroad car. I hauled it across the car, sparing a glance at my guest. He had gotten his boots off. His socks were a pile of threads on the floor.

I poured water into the tub and went back to the door. The Negro was gone.

"Goddammit!" I roared into the night.

I started to go out, back to the servant's car, but Donovan called, "Got any soap?"

I slammed shut the door and turned around.

He was naked. He was beautiful.

Long white legs, ropy muscles in his thighs. His abdomen pointed down, a perfect V, to point to the curly darker blond hair at his groin. His cock — his magnificent cock — even flaccid, was as long as the soles of his boots.

I stared at him. As I stared, I watched his cock grow more plump and straight.

He still stunk. That's what stopped me. The soap would help. I went to get the soap from my toilet.

I asked him, "Is that enough water?"

"It will be."

I heard him get into the tub, hissing as the water hit him. It was probably too hot, but I was not about to go out and dig up snow for him.

The soap smelled like mint as I held it to my nose, to get the stench of him out of it. I walked over and handed it to him.

He took it and rubbed it across his chest and arms. "Been too long since I've had a bath. Almost a year."

Yes, I was going to burn those clothes. "I may have something for you to wear," I said.

"If not, you'll have to keep me in this bathtub."

"I wouldn't mind that."

He laughed, cupped water with his hands and poured it over his head. He used the soap to lather up his hair and rinsed.

In the meantime, I stood and watched him. I watched his muscles bunch and stretch, his skin turn red, and then wrinkly, as he sat in the hot water that barely covered his hips. He scrubbed and scrubbed, going over himself two or three times. The rancid, dirty smell of him disappeared as the mint scent filled the room.

Finally, I let my hand drift down to the water. It was barely warm and yet he still sat in it. My hand touched his leg. He stopped moving, sitting completely still.

I moved my hand up from the middle of his thigh, up his leg toward his groin. His cock, soft when I watched him, immediately perked up as my hand drew closer to it. I entwined my fingers in his pubic hair, and he sat lower in the tub, thrusting his hips upward. I pulled back his foreskin and exposed his glistening head.

I rubbed my thumb around his head, tipping into the slit. He moaned and closed his eyes. Then I began to stroke him, slowly at first, feeling each bump of his cock with the inside of my index finger. He started to breathe a little heavier.

I continued to stroke, faster and faster. His breath came in rhythm to my stroking. His hips moved in the water, splashing me, my sleeve and jacket, but I didn't care. Then he stiffened, tensed, and I paused. As I did, I felt him swell in my hand, and he groaned as he arced a white ribbon of semen into the air, onto my sleeve, and added more spurts on my jacket and hand.

He lay back in the tub, his knees up against the other side of the tub. The water was cold now. His nipples were hard and pointed — whether from the water or his climax, I didn't know.

I smiled at him and took off my jacket.

My own cock pressed against my pants as I stood up. He watched me, then as I started to unbutton my shirt, he rose in the tub. It would be wonderful to take him.

He had a grin as he stepped over the tub rim and I got my shirt off. I wasn't as well-built as him; I was shorter and stockier, my hair darker, my skin olive. My blood came from the Greeks. Compared to him, I was an imp.

I said to him, "Have you ever done this before?"

"No," he said. "But I've heard about it."

"It's better than what you hear." Again, I grinned at him. *A virgin, as well!*

He walked over to me and pressed his hand against my swollen member. I groaned at the contact. His hands were already at my pants, and he unbuttoned the fly as I ground against his hand, wanting more of his touch.

He parted my cotton pants and my cock sprang out. He rubbed the palm of his hand against my head.

"Not here," I said. "I'm going to take you in bed."

"I think it's gonna be the other way around," he said.

I stopped short. In all my years, I had never been the one to receive. I was always in control. I took the top.

He picked me up, like I was nothing more than a sack of flour, and carried me to the bed.

"Wait," I said. "Wait a minute."

But he was caught in the throes of lust, as he stripped me of my pants.

I could have fought him off, but I wanted this god among men, this great Nordic creature. If it meant that I would allow him to control me, then so be it.

He lifted my arms above my head so I couldn't fight him, even if I wanted to.

I gave him token resistance, saying, "You have this all wrong."

"No," he said, "I think I got it right."

"Use the jelly in the nightstand. It'll be smoother."

He didn't seem to want to let go of my hands, in case I would wiggle out of his grasp.

"I'm not going anywhere," I said.

Donovan tilted his body and switched hands, holding me down as he pulled open the drawer of the nightstand. He rummaged around and found the petroleum jelly jar.

"Put some on your cock. Let me watch you."

He scooped some, a little too much, and smeared it over his cock. He stroked his member, covering it thoroughly.

"Now put some on your fingers and put it in my ass." I even tilted up my hips for him.

He looked confused for a moment, and then he did what I told him.

His fingers were large, and one finger in my virgin ass made me tighten up immediately.

"Again," I said, forcing myself to relax, to receive him. His cock was going to either hurt or be the most pleasurable thing I had ever known. I was going to make it the latter, even if I had to force myself.

When I got used to his one finger, I asked for more. He misunderstood, and pressed his cock against my hole. My eyes widened and, before I could stop him, he thrust forward.

The pain was intense, but pleasurable — something I never had before. He kept pushing forward as I writhed underneath him, both wanting it, and reflexively trying to deny him. He kept pushing forward, meeting resistance, but being relentless as he pressed inside me.

I relaxed and moved against him, my own cock sometimes striking against his abdomen as he lay above me. His hips thrust hard into me, and I felt the intensity building slowly, even as direct contact with my cock was denied. I wanted him to stroke me. I wanted him to touch me. But one hand held me down while the other hand held himself up.

He was lost in himself, so I couldn't talk to him. Instead, I allowed myself to stoke the fires within me. Every brush of his abdomen against my cock was a small spark that fed the fire. Closer and closer I came, until the sensitivity was too much.

"Ah, fuck," I heard him say and, at the same time, I shot along my abdomen with a cry of release. He bowed his head, pounded twice within me, and then tensed. He then climaxed as well.

He collapsed onto me as we both panted. I felt him slip out of me soon after, and he released my hands. I put them around him and held him like that until we both fell asleep, no more words being said.

9

The next morning, Sunday, I sent another Negro (not the same one as last night, as I had decided that, if I saw him again, I'd beat him senseless) to find clothes for Donovan. Helltown didn't have a cobbler, but a town a few miles away in Utah did. The train would be within riding distance of that town, so I sent the Negro with money and a horse to get boots for Donovan.

In the meantime, Donovan would be staying with me. Until he had clothes, I hid him in my bed while I had meetings with engineers and supervisors. It took a couple of days, but he finally had some clothes and I could send him back to work.

I didn't want to, but appearances were everything. As we approached the Summit, and I could see the $1,000 in my sights, I drove the men harder. I slept with Donovan only on Saturdays and, the rest of the time, we both understood that our relationship was of convenience. He never said a word of my constant submission and, as far as I knew, he never admitted submission either.

On May 8th, we arrived at Promontory Summit first. I won. Durant arrived a day later by stagecoach to congratulate me, but not give me my money. Central Pacific showed up on May 10, and we had a ceremony where the Central Pacific executive put in the last spike, though he missed on the first swing and almost slammed his foot. I stayed out of the picture.

I walked alone along the Central Pacific track. They had done an adequate job, though the Mormons on my side did a much better job, in my opinion. The sky was overcast, but the day was warm. I saw a hawk on the wind, circling above me, waiting for me to lie down and die so he could pluck out my eyes, no doubt.

"My Lady," I prayed quietly. "I have found my mate."

No, said a voice on the wind. *You have found your heir.*

I turned around in a circle, but saw only the hawk.

I knew I would die this time around.

As long as I got my $1,000 ...

TAURUS

OUTSIDE SPRINGFIELD, TEXAS
JUNE 17, 1949

I

ISAIAH FISHER LIVED ALONE ON THE PRAIRIE and that's just the way he liked it. However, the afternoon he got kicked in the ribs by one of the horses, he realized he needed a ranch hand.

Dr. Pike shook his head as he examined Isaiah's torso. "You're going to have a nasty bruise, but I don't think it's broken." He stood up. "You'd better marry you a sturdy wife."

Isaiah snorted. "Don't need no wife to nag me to hell."

"No, but someday one of those animals are going to crack your skull and bleed your brains out all over your goddamn barn."

Pike gathered his bag. He gave Isaiah a stern look, which a lesser man would have withered under.

But not Isaiah. He'd been through hell and back in the Pacific with those goddamn Japanese. This was his brother's ranch that he bought after a nasty fight with the rest of the family. A glare by the doctor was nothing.

Pike shrugged. "Suit yourself."

"Maybe a hand," admitted Isaiah.

"Plenty of Mexicans in town."

"Don't speak Mexican." Isaiah hauled himself out of the chair. "I'll put an ad in the paper."

He went down to the *Springfield Call* and put an ad in the newspaper. He hated that he had to pay money for it, but he didn't want to pick up some guy off the street — especially one of the Mexicans.

Three days later, Isaiah was saddling a horse in the barn when someone pounded on the wooden door. He led the horse to the door and opened it.

A dark-haired man stood in the doorway. He wore a cowboy hat, flannel shirt and jeans, and carried a green duffel bag that looked like Army issue.

"Hello," the man said.

Isaiah nodded to him.

"I'm here for the ad." The man showed Isiah the newspaper.

"Ever ride a horse?"

"Yes, sir."

Isaiah thumbed at the other horse in the barn. "Saddle up Sally. Come out with me to gather the cows."

He only had three cows, but they had plenty of land. He mostly had steer, getting them ready for the slaughter that would happen later on in the season. After rounding up the cows, he was going to mend fences.

Isaiah shifted from foot to foot, waiting for the man to saddle up the horse. He should be out in the field by now, he thought. Why did he have to wait for someone? This whole idea of an additional hand — an additional mouth to feed — was a stupid idea.

As he mounted the horse to get ready to leave the man behind, the man came out, leading the horse. Sally was docile and a slow, aged horse; while Miles, his own horse, was a faster, gilded stallion.

"C'mon," Isaiah said, and led the way out into the field.

The man said nothing but followed dutifully.

Isaiah could tell the man was experienced. He was able to easily guide the horse toward the cows and herd them toward the barn. When Isaiah closed the barn doors after the cows went in, he knew he had his man.

Isaiah gathered the items for fence repair. The man followed and they worked for the rest of the day in relative silence. A whole line of fencing had been knocked down, but twilight was approaching. They had gotten some of the posts up, but as for the slats, that would have to wait until tomorrow.

Normally he would go home, listen to something on the radio while making dinner, and fall asleep in his easy chair. Now, he would have to entertain a guest.

"Want me to make dinner?" the man asked.

Isaiah blinked in surprise before answering. "I got some ham in the icebox."

"Good enough," he answered, and spurred his horse forward, heading toward the house.

Isaiah went into the barn as the man had dismounted and removed the saddle. He brushed Sally before feeding her. Isaiah took his time with Miles as the man went to the house. Isaiah always left the doors unlocked, so the man could let himself inside.

After finishing with Miles, Isaiah went into the house. He found the man in the kitchen, slicing huge hunks of ham off the bone, laying out sandwiches. He put them on white plates that Isaiah hadn't seen in five years. He had found Maisy's fine china.

At that moment, Isaiah knew where the man would be sleeping. He had a cottage that had been used for Maisy's sons. Once Isaiah had bought out the ranch and kicked out Maisy and her kids, he had locked up the cottage and never went in it. For all he knew, it didn't have running water anymore.

The man sat at the kitchen table — again, somewhere that Isaiah himself never sat. He pulled out a chair and sat with the man.

"You don't have much to say," said the man, after taking a bite of his sandwich.

"There a problem with that?"

"Not with me."

They ate, then Isaiah brought the man out in the dark to the cottage. He flipped on the electricity to the house and let the man in.

It smelled old, musty, and unused. Inches of dust lined every corner.

The man said, "You want me to stay here?"

"Needs a little cleaning up, but the lights work."

Isaiah left the man standing in the doorway with his duffel bag over his shoulder. Isaiah didn't want to go into the cottage. He didn't want to know what the kids had left behind.

Isaiah went back to the house, shut the door, and leaned against it. He had done so well without another person in his life for so long.

Why did this handsome man have to show up now?

2

About a half hour after cock's crow, Isaiah heard a knock at his front door. He was half-awake, running on automatic pilot, and the knock snapped him out of his dream-like state. He remembered the day before ... the dark-haired handsome man who showed up to do work with him.

Was he still here?

Isaiah opened the door. The man wore a different shirt, but the same jeans as the day before. "What now?"

"Ever milk a cow?"

"It's been a few years."

"It's like riding a bike," said Isaiah. "I'll bring out breakfast. Meet you in the barn."

Breakfast was eggs and sliced tomatoes between two slices of toast. Most of the day passed in silence again while they milked, let the cows out, and headed out to the knocked-down fence.

This time, however, some steer were in the patch of land. Isaiah looked at the brand, and saw they belonged to McLaughlin, on the other side of the river. He had to go through another thousand acres to get to this part of his ranch. Did Jason know that Mac was using his land?

Isaiah, as a good neighbor, knew he should talk to Jason, warn him about Mac using his land.

"Not my problem," said Isaiah.

He started to try and shoo them across the broken-down fencing, back onto Jason's land. They merely stared at him.

The man knew what he was trying to do and got in closer to the steer. Slowly, in a clump, they started to move across the fence. They were a couple of yards away from the fence when the man returned. He and Isaiah tried to work quickly to get the fencing back up before the steer tried to knock it down again.

Finally, the man said to him, "My name is Peter."

"Isaiah."

Peter held out his hand. Isaiah looked at it for a long time, debating whether to take this step. Then he shook it.

Peter went back to work.

3

The dark-haired man had a name. He probably also had a history. That meant Isaiah would have to discuss his history. He didn't want to, especially about his time in the Navy that turned him from an optimistic young teenager to a bitter, bitter man.

It had all started on the *Iowa*. Petty Officer Charles Grace was handsome. With strong, chiseled features and broad shoulders, he easily lifted the torpedoes into their bays. Isaiah was too small for that, but he could get into the small places that other men couldn't get into and unblock or clean them.

Charles — never Charlie — took a liking to the young man. More than a liking to Isaiah. At night, while men grunted and groaned in their sleep on the hammocks, Charles approached young Isaiah. He let Isaiah know that sometimes men touched other men. That he was an adorable young man, attractive to Charles.

Charles wanted to show Isaiah how much he attracted him.

Isaiah was awake in his hammock when Charles approached him one evening. Charles caressed the young teenager, still with barely any hair on his small body. Charles' fingertips encircled a nipple, and Isaiah whimpered under the touch.

This seemed to be the effect Charles was looking for. Charles kissed Isaiah, who responded automatically, copying Charles' motions.

However, Charles did not want to be touched. He controlled the situation. He pulled Isaiah forward, divested him of his pants, and rubbed his own member against Isaiah. He didn't penetrate, but Isaiah felt the wetness as Charles grunted and shot along his back.

That was the first time. However, that was all it took. Charles returned, night after night, constantly touching Isaiah, holding Isaiah's hands up above his head while he rubbed against him. It didn't take long before Isaiah knew what Charles was preparing him for, so when Charles put the gag over Isaiah's mouth, Isaiah didn't protest. He screamed into the gag when Charles entered him — something that big didn't belong there, but it felt so good after the initial entry. And again, the next night. And again.

Isaiah shook his head to bring himself back to the present. No, he couldn't tell Peter how he loved the feeling at first. He couldn't tell him anything.

It was Saturday, and Isaiah had to ask him while they were coming back from herding the steers. "You a religious man?"

Isaiah planned to work on Sunday. He didn't keep the Lord's day. He had lost his religion years ago. But this was Texas, after all. Everyone was God-fearing here.

"I don't go to church," Peter said, looking down.

"Good. Neither do I." He glanced at the barn. "Gotta sort the cattle tomorrow. I thought I saw some of my neighbor's in there."

"Okay," said Peter, and turned Sally toward the entrance to the barn.

That night, Isaiah sat on the front porch, smoking a pipe. It was too nice of a night to stay inside. He looked up at the stars, trying to count them like he did when he was a child. That usually helped him to sleep.

He heard someone coming his way and turned his head. Peter stood at the foot of the porch steps, holding a bottle.

"I found this in the house. Do you drink wine?"

"I don't drink," said Isaiah, sitting up straight.

"Oh. Sorry, then."

Peter stayed there. He seemed to want to say something more. Isaiah knew the ball was in his court, whether to allow this man to step onto the porch and into his life.

It had been so lonely all these years.

"Well, then —"

"Peter —"

Both men stopped talking. Both men looked at each other. Did Peter know that Isaiah thought about him at night? Did Peter know that, behind Isaiah's eyes, Isaiah wanted him, like he had been wanted on the *Iowa*?

Scuttlebutt came down the pike, and it wasn't long before he heard the rumors that he was Charles' plaything. Men treated him like a child. He tried to respond to Charles, but Charles refused his advances. Then Charles discarded him like a used rag doll on the day they crossed the equator. Isaiah vowed that he would never want another person — man or woman — again.

But now, Isaiah knew.

"Sorry I bothered you," said Peter, and turned away like an Army soldier would.

Isaiah could have stopped him. But he didn't.

He looked back up at the sky, no longer being comforted by the lights, but mocked by the dark space between them.

4

The next morning, it was like nothing happened. They found three of the cattle belonging to Jason, and two that belonged to McLaughlin. Isaiah could have just brought the cattle to the fence and set them free back onto Jason's property without having to talk to the man.

Peter segregated the five steer in a separate pen. He patted the nose of one of them while he said, "You should find out who owns these."

"I know who does," Isaiah said.

"Call him?"

"Don't got their phone."

"Where do they live?"

Isaiah pointed northeast. "They're from that way. I'll go set 'em loose over there."

"There's two different brands."

"Not my problem."

"Want me to go tell the guy?"

Peter kept scratching the steer's nose. The steer had his eyes closed, satisfied with the attention.

Isaiah shrugged. It would be the first time in two years that he had contact with Jason; a little longer than that with McLaughlin.

"Maybe he's got some of your cattle."

That was possible. But, unlike McLaughlin, he didn't make a living off of his cattle. They were some extra money come slaughter.

"I gotta go into town anyway." He would have to buy more food for his new guest.

"You know, we never discussed pay."

"How much you lookin' for?"

Peter shrugged. "Room and board. Five dollars a week."

"Yeah, all right."

Peter smiled. He looked even more irresistible when he did that. Isaiah had to look away.

Isaiah had to dig out the extra saddle bags for Sally, now that he had to shop for two. They took the horses into town, even though there were more cars than horses.

Grainger's had everything he needed. Grainger knew Isaiah was not the talkative or dallying type, so he quietly and properly prepared Isaiah's order. Peter walked around the store, examining items that had been there for years, coated with a layer of dust.

"This is like the cottage," Peter said, setting down a bottle of oil.

Grainger popped his head up at Peter's voice. Isaiah pursed his lips and remained silent. Grainger glanced at Isaiah, then went back to filling the order. Isaiah knew the town knew how he had booted Maisy and her sons out of the ranch, and that he was not a man to be trifled with. Isaiah also knew that the town gossips would pull Peter aside and tell him stories of just what type of man Isaiah was.

They didn't know the half of it.

After getting the dry goods and packing the saddlebags on the horses, Peter asked, "So how do we talk to your neighbor? Isn't there an operator here in town that can connect you?"

"You can go to his place. I gotta bring this back to the house."

Peter opened his mouth to say something, but Isaiah mounted the horse and kicked Miles toward the road.

Just then a truck came barreling down the street, going much faster than the horse that stood in the middle of its path. There was nowhere for Isaiah and Miles to go.

Isaiah's last thought was, *I'm going to die without having known him.*

But as he thought it, a tremor erupted beneath him, knocking the horse off his feet. The horse tilted sideways, while Isaiah was tangled in the stirrups. Then the horse's body crashed down onto Isaiah's leg. Moments later, a huge stone wall erupted in the middle of the street.

Isaiah thought he heard the crunch of the truck slamming into it. Isaiah's leg was twisted and broken under Miles. Miles struggled to get up, but Peter arrived to help Isaiah out of the saddle and calm the horse. If the horse attempted to get up, he would drag Isaiah with him, and the damage would be much worse.

Then, the stone wall sank into the street — the only remnants of it a crushed truck and a line of dirt. People ran to the truck.

Peter pulled Isaiah clear of Miles. The horse struggled to stand. Peter put his hand to the horse's head, and the horse calmed down instantly, lying down. A puddle of blood was beneath the horse.

Isaiah leaned heavily on Peter as he got up.

Peter looked at the snapped leg, blood on the jeans, and an exposed bone. "Oh, God," he said.

Someone came and took Miles by the reins—the horse reared and stood, almost pulling the other man off his feet.

"It doesn't hurt," Isaiah said.

He glanced at the truck. The front grille was laminated across the engine, which had ended up on the male driver and female passenger's lap. He turned away as Peter pulled him from the scene.

He saw Dr. Pike go running up to the truck, but even Isaiah knew there was nothing the doctor could do for them.

Peter got Isaiah to sit down on a set of steps until Dr. Pike came over to them.

"You should go to the hospital," Pike said.

"Just set it," Isaiah said.

"It's not that easy."

"Dammit." Isaiah looked down at his leg. It really didn't hurt, but he was feeling lightheaded. "I saw worse in the war."

"Here's the ambulance."

Pike waved the car over to them. The driver bundled Isaiah into a gurney and drove him away, sirens blaring, leaving Peter behind with the horses.

5

Isaiah didn't remember when they set his leg, didn't remember how they put the cast on him, and didn't remember getting into the hospital bed until he woke up in it, his leg encased in a cast on a frame.

He twisted around in the bed, but he was very woozy.

"Hey, easy now," said a gentle voice from the other side of the room.

Isaiah lifted his head to see Peter in the doorway. "What're you doing here?" Isaiah asked him.

"Seeing to you. Doctors said you'll be here for a while. I don't know when I'll be able to get back."

A curtain separated him from the other side of the room. Isaiah could hear snoring next to him.

"Somebody's gotta milk the cows and see to the cattle while you're gone."

Isaiah looked up at the ceiling. He was not a man who cried, but he swallowed something, not tears. Something choked him up.

"That is, if you want me to."

Isaiah said, still looking up at the ceiling, "Can't afford to pay you."

"That's all right. I'll eat you out of house and home."

Isaiah snorted a laugh, turned to face Peter.

Peter stood next to the bed, looking at the leg in its cast. "When they let you go," he said, "I can help out with your leg."

"Might be weeks," Isaiah said. Just the thought depressed him.

"Won't be that long. I know how hospitals work. Once they find out you don't have the good insurance, they'll kick you out in days."

"How did you get here, anyway?"

"Mrs. Perch, your neighbor, let me borrow the car after I brought back their cattle."

"You did what?"

Peter looked down. "They weren't our cattle. And when I told her you were in the hospital ..."

How could she feel sorry for him when he had kicked out her neighbor of twenty years? He never talked to her in the three years he'd been at the ranch.

"Use the jalopy in the barn next time. Keys are in the house, in the cabinet above the sink."

"That truck has keys?" Peter laughed. "It's old enough to be a classic."

"It was my brother's," Isaiah said. He hardly used it because, after the war, he hated driving. "It might need gas."

"Okay," said Peter. He looked at Isaiah with a mixture of concern and relief. "It could have been much worse."

"Yeah, I know."

Peter reached out and touched the cast. Isaiah thought his bones could feel the touch. "You take it easy. They have the number to your house, right?"

"Yeah."

"Okay. I'll get the truck running and come to pick you up when they discharge you."

He pulled his hand back. Isaiah felt a tingle in his leg — an itch. But there was nothing he could do to scratch it.

6

A day later, he was on crutches and four hours after that, he was told he could go home.

Disgusted, Isaiah waved away the wheelchair and painfully hobbled down to the first floor, where Peter waited with the truck. Isaiah didn't think the hunk of junk in the garage was workable, but Peter stood there proudly next to it. He'd even washed it.

Peter let Isaiah struggle to get inside, then he slammed shut the metal door. Peter got in on his side, while Isaiah struggled to catch his breath. Peter watched, concerned.

"Go," said Isaiah. "Get me the hell outta here."

Peter put the clutch in and eased the truck out of the circular drive of the hospital. He drove slowly — too slow for Isaiah's taste — but he knew that Peter went slowly on his account, so as to not jar his leg unnecessarily. Isaiah didn't care. He wanted to go home, settle in his own house, his own bed, with his own food, and the familiar smells of the farm around him.

Taking the long way, but with less dirt roads, Peter got him home after an hour. Isaiah hadn't said a word the entire time.

Peter parked the truck close to the house and turned to Isaiah. "You're going to let me help you out."

Isaiah looked at the steps up to his front door. There were steps to the back door, but the idea of getting to the back without tripping over something seemed impossible. Isaiah threw open the door.

Peter got out as Isaiah swung his leg out, letting it dangle. It was going to hurt like hell jumping down to the ground.

Then, the next thing he knew, Peter was there, putting his hands on Isiah's waist. He eased Isaiah to the ground so that it was a light touch on his leg.

Isaiah stared at Peter. Peter stared back. Isaiah wondered if Peter could see what he was doing to him — if he could see or feel the tightening of his jeans.

Peter didn't let go of Isaiah's waist for what seemed like a long time. Peter gulped, slid his hands from Isaiah's waist and wiped his hands on his worn jeans. Peter stepped away, giving Isaiah room.

He sighed without meaning to, making Peter jerk his head up. Isaiah grabbed his crutches. Without looking at Peter, he started to struggle up the steps. Peter stayed behind him, probably to catch him if he fell. He wouldn't fall. He refused to fall into the man's arms.

He made it to the top stair. Peter unlocked the door for him.

"You locked the door?"

"Habit," said Peter.

Isaiah grunted, and hauled himself into the house. Some things had been moved, giving him room to maneuver through the living room to the kitchen. The stairs leading upstairs looked difficult to climb with the crutches, but he would get up there no matter what.

"Coffee?" asked Peter.

"Yeah."

Peter started the percolator on the stove.

"First thing," said Isaiah. "I want to get out of these clothes and take a goddamn shower."

"You're going to need help with that."

"Yeah, I guess."

"You can't put the cast in the water. It'll dissolve."

"How do you know?"

"I've seen it happen," he said, and turned to the coffee on the stove. The smell of it made Isaiah's mouth water.

"Do I have any food left?" he asked.

"I got some eggs, and some sausages from next door."

"That sounds good."

The food smelled delicious while it cooked. Isaiah had pain pills, but he refused to take it. A little pain — okay, a lot of pain — was nothing. Peter silently cooked a couple of eggs and two sausages, grilling some toast to go with it. Even though it was dinnertime, breakfast for dinner made him almost smile. His mother did this often when money was tight and the chickens lay way too many eggs.

Peter didn't cook like his mother, but the food was good. However, the pain grew as he ate, and he didn't finish it.

"Is it all right?"

"Leg hurts," Isaiah said, rubbing his knee.

Peter frowned and set down his fork. "Do you want me to help you with that?"

"What can you do?"

"I can help heal your leg."

Isaiah shook his head. "You one of those faith healers?"

Peter seemed to blush. "You could say that."

"I don't believe in that. It doesn't work if you don't believe, that's what the preacher says."

"The preacher and I differ. You don't have to believe for it work. I was a combat medic in the war."

"You seen worse than broken legs."

"A lot worse. Things that I can't bring a man back from."

Isaiah reached for his crutches. "I'm gonna go to bed instead."

He winced as he stood up. The pain almost made him cry, but he refused to. He would tough it out.

Peter again stayed behind him as he climbed the stairs. He was bathed in sweat by the time he got to the top, and decided against the shower. Instead, he hobbled into the bathroom and shut the door to take a piss. When he came out, Peter held out the bottle of pills.

"These will at least help you sleep."

"You sayin' this as a combat medic?"

"I'm saying this as someone who doesn't like to see another man in pain."

Isaiah snatched the bottle from him and turned around so he wouldn't see his eyes well up. He took the pill and placed the bottle in the medicine cabinet.

By then, Isaiah had gathered himself together and was able to get to his bed.

"Let me know if you need any help," Peter said, and left the doorway.

Isaiah watched him go, half wanting him to help him out of his clothes and climb into bed with him.

He was able to get his shirt and shoes off before he collapsed, saying to himself, *Just a minute, I'll close my eyes ...*

7

Isaiah dreamed of floating on a raft, something the Navy did to prepare their men for austerity, but he wasn't alone. Peter was in uniform, an Army man's uniform, with the red cross band on his arm signifying he was a medic. The sea was calm. They were well within sight of land, and it was a beautiful warm day.

"You feel okay?" Peter asked.

Isaiah looked down at his leg that Peter held. It was bare, white, the wound where the bone had stuck out a dark red line across his shin. Peter moved his hand up and down his leg, caressing it. It felt like it was buoyed by the same water they were on. However, water didn't come out of Peter's hands, but green light. It seemed to burrow into his leg, floating with the bone, setting it, healing it — all without pain.

"I've healed the bone," said Peter. "Tomorrow I'll heal the muscles."

Isaiah reached for Peter. Peter gave him his hand and leaned forward.

"Don't leave me," Isaiah said, words he had used years ago with Charles.

Peter bent his head and kissed Isaiah, as gentle as brothers.

"Never."

8

Isaiah heard the cock's crow and bolted out of sleep. He was late. He swung his legs off the bed and started to get up, but his wounded leg didn't support him. He crashed to the floor, taking the ceramic wash basin with him down onto his head.

He lay stunned. The wash basin didn't break over his head, but his head felt broken. He put his hand to the back of his head: no blood. Isaiah turned over, the pain in his leg almost unbearable. It was chilly — he realized he was naked.

He heard someone coming up the stairs. He reached up, grabbed the sheet, and pulled it down seconds before the door opened. He looked upside down at Peter, standing there with a tray.

"What happened?" Peter asked.

He looked around the room, and placed the tray on the nightstand, pushing over an alarm clock.

"I fell," said Isaiah, struggling to sit up, hoping that the sheet covered him.

"I can see that."

Peter bent and pulled Isaiah up by his shoulders. His hands followed the contour of his body to his legs, where he cupped beneath the knees and lifted him as easily as he lifted a bag full of potatoes. Peter placed Isaiah gently on the bed, but the pain made Isaiah wince slightly.

Peter helped him sit up in bed, and then presented him with the tray of food. "Don't worry, I'm not going to do this every day."

Isaiah cracked open the soft-boiled egg and dipped the toast into its runny texture. "I don't know how I'm going to pay you back for all this."

"I'm sure I'll think of something," Peter said with a wink before leaving the room.

9

"You are one stubborn man," Peter said as Isaiah forced himself to hobble to the barn over the uneven terrain. "Don't you trust me?"

"I don't trust anyone anymore," Isaiah said, leaning on the crutch. He threw open the door to the barn.

There were the three cows in their stalls, eating hay, as quiet and as comfortable as if he'd done it himself.

"What about the bull?"

"He's out to pasture. Which one of these do you want pregnant?"

Isaiah hobbled up and down the row. He pointed at one of the cows. "Lynn's due."

"I'll set her out tomorrow."

Isaiah walked through the barn to the field. Everything looked fine. The bull wandered alone in his field; the steer were out in their fields.

"I gave the steer back that didn't belong to us. One of them claims not to have any of ours, but I don't believe him."

Isaiah stared at Peter. "Our steer?"

Peter blushed. "Sorry."

Isaiah wasn't sure what to think at that moment. He loved the idea that Peter thought of them as together, but didn't know if it was an assumption on Peter's part. Isaiah thought it best to say nothing. He turned from Peter and walked back to the house.

"Look, um, Isaiah ..."

Isaiah stopped between the house and barn.

"I know you're probably thinking that I'm trying to take over your place. I'm not."

Isaiah leaned on the crutches, listening.

"This is going to sound stupid," Peter said, looking down at the ground.

Not any more stupid than how I feel about you, Isaiah thought.

"I have to help people. It's in my nature. It's part of what makes me what I am."

"A combat medic?"

He shook his head. "An immortal."

Isaiah blinked. "What?"

Peter sighed. "I'm an immortal and, in order to stay that way, I have to help people." He motioned to Isaiah's leg. "And heal them if they're hurt. I caused your injury."

Isaiah remembered the wall of stone that had burst up out of the street. He had thought he imagined it. He thought the horse had gotten spooked from the car. The stone seemed to have slipped his mind until that very moment.

"The wall," Isaiah said.

"You remember. Most people forget stuff like that. I didn't know what else to do to stop that car."

"Are they —"

"They are."

"So you gotta, what ... atone, I guess? Do penance?"

"It's not like that." He started walking to the house. "You'd better sit down."

Isaiah got back to the house and sat down on the wicker chair on the porch. Peter leaned against the railing, his hands in his pockets, looking down at the well-worn wooden floor.

"A long time ago," he said. "I was a bullfighter."

"How long ago?"

Peter looked up.

"1682. In Spain." When Isaiah didn't react, Peter continued, "I was gored by a bull and died. Then a goddess brought me back to life."

"Goddess? Not God?"

He shook his head. "I never saw God. I was a Christian, and I thought it was the Virgin Mary. But it's another goddess. Her name is Ishtar. You probably never heard of her."

"No, I haven't."

Peter shrugged. "Anyway, she brought me to life, and told me that I had to help people. She gave me, I don't know...abilities? To work with animals and to heal people." Peter stood up straight. "In a couple of wars, I worked with the cavalry until they stopped using horses. The last war, I was the combat medic. I healed people that could be healed, but some people, like I said before, they were beyond healing."

"You tried to heal my leg last night."

"Yes. But I didn't want to heal it all at once. It takes a lot out of both me and you to do it."

"Me? Don't I just lie there?"

Peter laughed. "No. Here's where it gets crazy. Everything living has energy. You do, I do, the grass does-- everything. I use your energy to heal you, and I use my energy to tell it how to heal you." Peter tilted his head. "Does that make any sense?"

"Nope," Isaiah said. "But it works?"

"Yes."

"How fast?"

"I can have you walking with a cane tomorrow, and back on a horse the next day. It takes some time."

"Does it hurt?"

"Probably not any more than it does now."

"What do I need to do?"

Peter dropped to his knees. Isaiah's eyes widened—it was a position he had assumed on the *Iowa* too many times. He felt himself start to swell in the jeans and hoped to God that Peter didn't notice.

"Just relax."

Peter wrapped his hands around his shin. His leg was thick and strong from walking and riding, so Peter couldn't complete the circuit with his hands. Peter closed his eyes, and Isaiah started to feel warmth around Peter's hands.

This must be what it's like for a faith healing, Isaiah thought.

The warmth spread from where Peter's hands contacted his skin to someplace deeper, into his very bones.

Peter caressed his leg slowly, spreading the thick warmth down it, and making him even harder in his jeans.

He wanted to shift to adjust himself, but didn't dare move under Peter's hands. Peter got to the top of his boot, and then stroked upward slowly. Isaiah took a gasping breath, imagining him doing that to his cock.

Peter slipped his hands from his leg, and Isaiah found himself staring down at Peter, who stared at Isaiah's crotch.

"I'm sorry I did that to you," Peter said, his voice quiet.

"It's not your fault," said Isaiah.

Peter brought his hand up and pressed it against Isaiah's crotch.

Isaiah involuntarily moaned. Peter's hand was still hot with energy, and feeling that burn against his crotch made Isaiah even more hard.

"I'll take care of it for you," Peter said, unbuttoning the jeans.

Isaiah's breath came faster as Peter pushed down the underwear and exposed his cock to the open air.

Peter stroked him the same way he stroked his leg — slow and deliberate, his hand burning with heat and filling his cock. Isaiah spread his legs wider for him to get closer.

Peter moved his head close to Isaiah's cock, but didn't touch it. Isaiah hissed a moment, as a wave came over him, and he knew he was close and wouldn't be able to stop the next one. He gripped the arms of the chair tightly, holding himself back.

But Peter didn't stop, and when Peter's breath on Isaiah's head struck him, Isaiah lost all control. He exploded, covering Peter's face with white ribbons. Peter sighed, contented, as he let Isaiah shoot all over him.

Isaiah suddenly glared at Peter. "So that's the kind of shit you did in the Army?"

Peter sat back. "I —"

Isaiah stuffed himself back in his pants, still glaring with what he hoped was pure anger, but what he felt was pure lust. "Don't do that shit."

Peter untucked his own shirt. Isaiah could see the bulge in Peter's jeans as he rose, wiping his face on the hem of his shirt. "Sorry, Isaiah, I thought — I don't know."

"Yeah, well, you thought wrong."

"Sorry," he said again, his head down. "I'll be going."

Isaiah said nothing, not wanting to betray his own feelings. He wanted to say, *Stay with me.*

Instead, he stood up. He could put weight on the leg, but not long enough to walk on his own.

He grabbed one crutch, leaned on that, and stormed into the house. He slammed shut the door, closed his eyes and exhaled a captured sob.

10

After almost no sleep, Isaiah, still conflicted, rose from his bed two hours before dawn. After what happened yesterday, he didn't know if he should make breakfast for Peter. Hell, maybe Peter wasn't around.

He peered out the bedroom window at the cottage next door. The lights were on downstairs in the kitchen area. *Maybe he got just as little sleep as I did,* Isaiah thought. Or maybe not, and Peter always woke up before dawn.

Isaiah took a crutch and leaned on it as he went slowly down the stairs in the dark, putting on a light only in the bathroom. That light could easily be seen from the cottage's kitchen.

The next light was the kitchen area. The light from there bled into the living room, which could be seen from the kitchen in the cottage. Was Peter watching him hobble his way through the house?

He started brewing the coffee as the sky lightened from black to gray. He had just put toast in the toaster when there was a knock on the door.

It had to be Peter.

"Come in," Isaiah called. Peter opened the door and stepped inside. He carried the Army duffel that he had first showed up with.

"Isaiah, about last night."

Peter looked exhausted, with heavy bags under his blue eyes.

"I'm sorry about what I did. If you want me to go ..."

"I need a hand around here. You know what you're doin'." Isaiah thought the best thing to do would be to avoid discussing the topic at all. That way his body or his voice wouldn't disclose how he really felt.

"You sure?"

"Yeah, I'm sure. Go put your shit back and let's go milk the cows."

"Thanks, Isaiah."

The coffee percolator bubbled loudly. Isaiah turned to glare at it, but it had saved him from seeing Peter's reaction when he left the house.

II

It started to rain just after they milked the cows. They went out in the pouring rain to gather the steer from the fields. Again, Perch and McLaughlin's cattle were mixed in with his. McLaughlin's cattle looked sickly and mal-nourished. They trudged along with the other cattle, as if even lifting their hooves to walk was an effort.

Peter frowned under his hat. "Those don't look good."

"Leave 'em out here."

"I can't do that," Peter said, and looped them into the rest of the cattle.

"What they got they'll give to the other ones," Isaiah yelled.

"Not if I can help it," Peter said, riding out of earshot of Isaiah.

Great, Isaiah thought. *My food, my medicine, going to help someone else's cattle. Just what I need.*

Peter knew what he was doing. He kept the steer segregated so that they would not infect any other cattle. He fed them fresh grass that he cut himself. But most strange of all, he performed a faith healing on them, like he had done with Isaiah.

For two days, the steer didn't seem to respond to the treatment. How could they? They were dumb animals. They didn't understand a faith healing. On the third day, a car pulled into the driveway of his house.

Isaiah glared with a look that would make the car burst into flames. Peter came out of the barn leading the three sickly steer. Billy Mclaughlin, his diagonally-across neighbor, stepped out of the car.

Isaiah hadn't seen him in years. Billy had a gut on him and was going bald. Isaiah wondered if he looked that old.

"I have no idea how they got on your land," Billy said to Isaiah, as Isaiah limped down the stairs.

His leg was much better, but not ready to hold his full weight.

"We can keep them," said Peter.

Isaiah and Billy stared at Peter. "What the hell you gonna do with 'em?" demanded Isaiah.

"We can still use them."

"They're sick," said Isaiah.

Billy waved his hand. "Keep 'em. I don't care."

Peter led them back into the barn as Isaiah said, "Of course you don't care. They're gonna make my steer sick. You think you're gonna buy this land out from under me?"

Billy blinked. "Whoa, Isaiah, where are you getting that idea?"

It was something he wouldn't put past the man. He owned land throughout Springfield, through ill-gotten gains, if the rumors were true.

"I don't want to talk to you," Isaiah said, turning away. "You deal with Peter."

When he got to the bottom step, he heard the roar of the car's engine as it turned around in the driveway and headed out. Also, he wondered why he gave up dealing with his neighbors to Peter.

It looked like Peter was going to be sticking around a little longer. He looked up at his doorway, thinking pleasant thoughts about that idea.

12

The three steer were re-branded that afternoon, and Peter put his time in with them in earnest. Isaiah watched over the next few days. Peter didn't stop working with Isaiah, but any time there was free time, he spent it with the steer.

It worked. In a week, the steer were muscular and fatter, no longer rheumy-eyed, but clear and strong.

Sunday morning, Isaiah woke up to hear yelling outside. He went to the second bedroom, which looked out at the field near the barn.

Peter stood in the center of the field, one hand on his hip, the other holding a red sheet. He stood absolutely still, except for the billowing of the red sheet as he shook it vigorously.

Opposite him stood one of the steer, nose pointed to the ground, and pawing at it. Isaiah gasped. Was Peter crazy?

Isaiah turned to the stairs and tried to run down them, but he still couldn't put his weight on the leg. He heard Peter yell something that sounded like "Olay!" Isaiah barreled out the back door, the door closest to the field.

Now the steer was on the opposite side of the fence, again, threatening, pawing the ground. The steer stalked sideways. Peter pivoted his body with miniscule movements of his feet, always facing the steer.

Then the steer rushed at Peter.

"Peter!" yelled Isaiah, running to the fence.

Peter deftly stepped aside, ignoring Isaiah's cry, concentrating entirely on the steer heading his way. He lifted the red sheet and the steer stormed under it. The red sheet draped over the steer, while Peter yelled, "*Olé!*"

Peter glanced at Isaiah. Peter smiled, returned his attention to the steer who looked ready for another pass.

Isaiah stood at the fence, watching the steer run under the red sheet twice more. Isaiah's heart was in his throat each time the animal came within inches of goring Peter.

Then Peter folded the sheet and bowed. The steer straightened up and snorted. It was a game to them. They were both playing a game!

Peter went up to the steer and patted his head, then jumped over the fence to come up to Isaiah.

"Are you crazy?" Isaiah said. "That bull could have killed you."

"We had an agreement," Peter said with a smile.

"You can *talk* to them?"

Peter only kept smiling. He patted Isaiah's shoulder, then walked back to the cottage.

Isaiah shivered. That touch — could there be more coming from him someday?

13

They went into town the next day. Grainger again filled the order. His daughter, Becky, started talking to Peter. The two laughed and had a long conversation that Isaiah couldn't hear.

It didn't matter. The fire in his chest was unfamiliar whenever he heard the two laughing. It burned and made him even more sour with Grainger.

Mrs. Perch came into the store. "Mr. Fisher!" she cried to Isaiah.

Isaiah grunted in reply.

"Where is that nice young man — oh, there he is! Peter!" Mrs. Perch found her way to Peter. "Peter! I know you don't belong to the community parish, but we are having a Four-H this Sunday after services. I would hope you could find your way to come."

Isaiah never went to the Four-H meetings. They existed only to show off everyone's livestock. He didn't raise livestock for showing off; he raised them for food.

"Only if Isaiah is invited, too."

Mrs. Perch whipped around to Isaiah. Isaiah hid his shock well, he thought.

"Well, er, of course."

"Good! We'll both be there."

Isaiah narrowed his eyes as Mrs. Perch left the store, giving Isaiah the side-eye as she went by.

"What makes you think I'll go to any Four-H?" asked Isaiah.

"Because I'm going, and I'm bringing Charlie to show off."

"Charlie?" Isaiah almost choked the word out. Of all the names in the world he could have picked ...

"The bull you saw me with a couple of days ago. We've been practicing."

Grainger looked from one man to the other. Isaiah waved a hand in dismissal and walked out with his full saddlebags.

14

Sunday arrived. Isaiah was in his usual work clothes, while Peter was in a bleached and starched button-down shirt and black pants.

"You're going to church?" asked Isaiah.

"I was hoping you would come."

"Church don't mean nothing to me."

"It doesn't mean anything to me, either, but I need someone to watch Charlie."

"I'm gonna babysit your goddamn bull?"

"You can always go to church and I'll babysit my goddamn bull."

Isaiah muttered darkly, "I don' even wanna go see this Four-H."

"Come on, you'll have fun. Free food."

Isaiah saddled the horse.

15

It ended up that Charlie had his own pen and there were some young teenagers who volunteered to watch the animals. Isaiah glowered as he walked into the church, ignoring the preacher who greeted him. Peter shook hands with the man, though, as if to apologize for Isaiah's lack of social graces.

They took spots in the back of the church. Isaiah could not hide his disgust at the way the people acted in church, all holier-than-thou, and how they acted with him.

They passed the plate. Peter put in a whole dollar while Isaiah passed it on without giving anything. This church didn't look like it needed the money.

"Relax," whispered Peter as they stood up to sing a hymn.

Isaiah had to go to church services on the *Iowa*, and the more he was forced to go, the angrier he got at the chaplain. The chaplain knew about Charles and Isaiah. The chaplain mentioned it once, before Charles tossed Isaiah aside. After Charles hurt him, the chaplain didn't step forward to help. No one did.

So he built walls.

16

After the service, Isaiah went directly to Charlie's pen. Compared to some of the other bulls, Charlie wasn't a spectacular specimen. But he was better than he had been when they first got him from Mclaughlin.

Billy Mclaughlin came over to Isaiah. "That one is one of those sick ones I gave you?"

"Yes," said Isaiah, watching Peter feed the bull and pat the middle of his forehead.

"Maybe they weren't so sick after all."

"They were damn sick," said Isaiah. "Peter took care of 'em."

"He a veterinarian?"

"No. He just knows what he's doing."

"Ah," said Billy. Then he called to Peter, "Hey, Pete, how much this tightwad paying you?"

Isaiah balled his hands into fists, almost ready to punch him.

"Name's Peter," he said. "And you couldn't pay me enough."

Isaiah felt his heart grow, something he hadn't felt in years. Pride.

"You sure? I'll bet I could. I need someone like you."

Peter shook his head, and went back to petting Charlie.

"You heard the man," said Isaiah.

"You wait."

Isaiah walked away from Billy to join Peter. Peter smiled at Isaiah. "I wouldn't leave you."

Isaiah looked at the ground. He couldn't bring himself to say anything in response.

After the horses pranced around a field, Peter was able to get the use of the field with Charlie. A crowd gathered at the fence to watch Peter stand alone in the middle of the field. Someone opened the stockade and Charlie flew out of it, into the field.

"Toro!" yelled Peter, waving the red sheet wildly.

The bull turned. He snorted and went at Peter. The entire crowd, including Isaiah, gasped as the running bull approached Peter.

At the last second, Peter stepped aside and the bull brushed the sheet. "*Olé!*" yelled Peter, turning to face the bull.

After a few times of this, the kids started yelling, "*Olé!*" whenever Peter's red sheet caressed the rushing bull. The purpose of this game was to tire out the bull, to see who had more endurance.

Then, someone's young girl ran out into the field.

Peter was distracted. The bull went at him, and Peter didn't move away in time. The bull's horns slammed into Peter, carrying him a couple of feet, and then the bull threw Peter over his head. An arc of blood followed.

Isaiah ran out and grabbed the red sheet. "Toro!" he yelled, getting the bull's attention.

He led the bull toward the stockade, placing the red sheet in front of it, and the bull ran into it, slamming into the fence, being stunned for a moment.

Then there was a gunshot, and the bull fell where it stood.

Isaiah didn't even look to see who shot the bull, but turned to see the crowd that had gathered around the prone body of Peter. Isaiah fought his way through.

His white shirt was stained crimson all the way up to his chest. Isaiah bent and picked up Peter's head. Peter opened his eyes.

"Peter," whispered Isaiah, "I'm so sorry."

Peter raised his right hand, covered in blood, and placed it on Isaiah's cheek.

"*Vi amor en tus ojos,*" Peter said. His eyes unfocused, and the blue light behind them faded out.

Dr. Pike came through the crowd as Isaiah placed Peter's head down.

Vi amor en tus ojos.

He would never forget those words for as long as he lived.

"I'm sorry, Isaiah," said Pike.

Isaiah picked up the body. He brought Peter to his horse, and lay him across it, tying him down.

"Mr. Fisher, we can put him in my truck —"

Isaiah heard nothing but Peter's voice.

Vi amor en tus ojos.

He had no idea what it meant, but it must have been Spanish, since he said he was originally from Spain.

Before he got back to his land, he stopped in Springfield and approached some Mexicans. They stared at the body on the horse, crossing themselves as they looked upon it.

"What does '*Vi amor en tus ojos*' mean?" he demanded of the group of Mexicans gathering around.

A woman stepped forward, touched Isaiah's leg on the stirrup. "It means, 'I saw the love in your eyes.'"

Tears flowed down his cheeks, wholly unexpected. He jerked on the horse's reins and turned him to the ranch.

17

The next day, Mr. Perch went to Isaiah's house to see if he needed help with the grave for the nice young man. He discovered Isaiah dead in his bed, an empty bottle of laudanum on the nightstand.

Peter's body lay beside Isaiah.

They were buried together.

VIRGO

CHICAGO, ILLINOIS
MAY 13, 1930

I

JOEY "NEEDLES" ESPOSITO HAD BETTER THINGS TO DO than to go to the flower shop. His brother had just died, and he needed to be home with his mother. But Big Al wanted to send flowers, and this florist didn't have a phone.

"Let me pay for your family's flowers," said Big Al. "It's the least I can do."

So Needles parked the car outside of Irv's Flowers on Division Street in Chicago. A Jew in the north side of Chicago, where Al Capone and the Outfit controlled the street? That was some serious balls — or he had something on everyone.

Needles walked into the place. A bell tinkled above the door daintily, not angrily like a butcher shop's. He frowned, which made him look, and feel, more ticked off at this stupid errand. Why didn't this guy have a phone?

"Be right with you," came a voice from the back of the store.

Needles looked around. He smelled the pungent roses, the deep earth of the greens; saw tulips, lilies, and carnations everywhere. He saw other flowers that he couldn't name.

"Sorry about that," said the man's voice, now near him.

Needles stood in front of a glass counter. The man who came out from a curtained area to stand behind the counter was small, black-haired, and looked more Italian than Jewish. His hair was cut short, over his ears, and he wore glasses.

He wiped his hands on a blue apron. "What can I get for you?"

"Flowers for my brother, Jimmy."

His face saddened. "I'm sorry to hear that." He took out a pad and licked the pencil end. "Roses, carnations?"

Needles shrugged.

"Open casket or closed casket?"

"Open." Mama knew the undertaker had his work cut out for him, but he was lucky they hadn't blown his face off.

"At home or in one of those parlors?"

"One of those parlors."

"Do you know which one?"

"Not The Mick."

"McCain's?" The man looked up and smiled at Needles. "You're with Capone's boys?"

"My brother was."

"And what about you?"

Needles shrugged again. Was this guy a cop or something?

The florist sighed and scribbled a few things on the paper. "Just want to know who's paying the bill."

"The Outfit."

The florist finished writing, then tore off the top sheet. Underneath was a purple sheet, which he tucked under the pad. He tore off the next sheet, folded it, and put it in an envelope.

"This is the bill. When's the funeral?"

"Coupla days."

"You're a man of few words. What's your name?"

"Needles." He took the envelope.

The man nodded. "Needles. Give that to the accountant and he'll know what to do. I hope to see you again, under better circumstances."

"Yeah."

Needles hoped not.

2

Needles drove home. His mother was already in black, women gathered around her in the kitchen, non-stop cooking. He kissed them all: his aunts and extended family. The men were in the other room, smoking and talking.

Needles checked on his mother, kissing her last.

"Is everything all right?"

"Everything is mostly all right," she said.

His father had disappeared, probably already at the bar. He wouldn't be surprised.

Needles went into the living room. He stopped at the entrance to take a look at the men. All of them were wiseguys from the Outfit. Needles wasn't the only one left in the family who could go and work for Capone. It looked like they were going after his youngest brother, Timothy.

"Hey," said Trevino, suddenly appearing next to Needles. He clapped Needles on the back. "Sorry about your brother."

Needles shrugged.

"You ordered the flowers?"

"Yeah, they'll be at the funeral parlor. I didn't remember the name of the place."

"That's all right. We just started using it."

"I don't think my mother could take dealing with Johnny being here in the house."

"Your father sure as hell can't." This came from one of the other heavyset men who had a cigar in his mouth. He chomped on the end of it and blew the smoke up in the air out of Needles' face. "I think he ran away."

"My father doesn't like that we work with you guys."

"Then he's not going to get anywhere further than the garbage man he already is. You, kid, you're going to get far."

Needles wondered if he was going to get as far as his brother.

As the women served the men dinner, Needles watched how they acted around Timothy. Timothy looked like he was ready to join them. Needles was already deep enough to be noticed, but he was still considered young at twenty-two. His mother was Italian, and understood how the Outfit belonged to the family. His father, well, he wasn't Italian. He was "a mutt" — a mix of English and French Canadian.

Needles loved his mother's side of the family. They fed him and made him feel important. Uncle Trevino had introduced him into the Outfit right away. He was seven, and already in fights. Needles fought often enough to be noticed. He used his fists, not a gun.

Johnny used a gun. That got him in trouble, Needles knew. Guns versus guns never worked out.

The men stayed late, well after midnight, drinking and talking, smoking and eating. Mama finally collapsed in a chair and his aunts kicked everyone out. Needles and Timothy went to bed.

He lay his head on the pillow, and thought he could smell roses. He checked under the pillow, but there was nothing. He roughed up the pillow and rested his head on it again. Roses. Light and gentle, but still there.

3

His dream was full of roses. Needles found himself walking in a park, a place that didn't exist in the real world, but somewhere that he had imagined when he was young. The park was overgrown with flowers. Scents of juniper and pine mixed with the roses and lavender.

He walked on a path, and it diverged into two at the base of a large oak tree. He tried to look down the path, to see where they led. One path led into thickets and seemed like a dead end. The other path led into a meadow. He chose that path.

The grass was up to his chest around the path, as he walked in the bright meadow. Someone came up the path to meet him. He was smaller than Needles. Bald, but with a pony tail on the top of his head, and he wore only a skirt.

This was a strange man he had never seen before in his dreams. As he got closer, the man started to look familiar. The man's face niggled at the corners of his mind: a man he should have known, but didn't.

The man came up to Needles. He smelled again of deep red roses. Needles breathed deep of the scent.

Then the man touched Needles' chest. Needles' clothes fell away, and he stood naked before this man. He felt himself stirring, getting hard. The man was muscular, but not as much as Needles. The man's hand moved around Needles' chest and pulled him into a hug. The feeling of the man's muscular chest against his own was too much to bear.

Needles gave in — it was a dream, after all — and grabbed the man's pony tail, pulling his head up. Needles kissed the man, hard and rough, and the man shuddered beneath him. The man's skirt fell down into a pile at his feet, and Needles felt the hot cock of the man press against his own.

The man's hands wandered along Needles' body, squeezing and rubbing, until Needles grabbed his hand and placed it on his own cock.

Needles moaned, heard himself audibly moan in his sleep, as he woke up feeling himself shoot in his own bed.

"Fuck," he whispered, shuddering in the cold wetness of the bed.

4

Johnny's funeral was uneventful. Needles did notice, however, the flowers in the parlor, the thick scent of roses. It almost made Needles hard in his pants as the scents brought him back to the dream.

His parents were in black. He wore a suit one size too small, and Timothy looked like an undertaker in his dark blue suit, one that had belonged to Johnny.

Needles did look at the flowers. They were beautifully arranged, Tasteful, not too much green, but real flowers:

carnations, roses and lilies. Women found them beautiful. At the gravesite, they took some for a remembrance.

At first, Needles was going to go with his father to the bar, but Capone's men asked him to come along with them.

His cousin pulled him aside and said, "I know it's right after your brother's funeral, but we got a job that he didn't finish and Mr. Capone thought you could do it."

Needles stood up straighter. If Mr. Capone was involved, he would do it.

"There's a guy who hasn't been paying us lately. Can you go remind him to pay us?"

"Yeah," Needles said. "Who's the guy?"

"Next to the flower shop you went to a couple days ago. It's a bicycle shop."

"Want me to take care of it now?"

"If you could," said his cousin, as he rubbed the back of his head. "Think you could do it by yourself?"

"How hard can it be?"

"I'll get Ronnie to bring you there."

His cousin introduced him to Ronnie, a thin man who looked like he could get blown over by a stiff wind. They got into Ronnie's car and took off. He didn't go to the reception with his mother. He wouldn't be missed for the few minutes it was going to take him.

5

Needles walked into the bike shop and noticed the first weapon he could use, an air pump. It was a tube made of steel. One end was metal with square edges meant to put your feet on, and the other end had the pump. A rubber tube led from the pump to a copper end which hung loosely from the bottom.

The man behind the counter was easily as old as his grandfather, bald, clean-shaven, wrinkled and stooped.

"Can I help you?"

"I'm from the Outfit." Needles picked up the air pump.

The man behind the counter did nothing. Needles swung it carelessly and its bottom edge slammed into the glass counter, shattering it.

Now the man jumped back, and Needles saw someone running in from the back room. A young woman in overalls, her hands and coveralls were covered in grease.

"Papa —"

"Sarah, get back."

Needles grinned at her. "Yeah, this doesn't involve you."

"Hell it doesn't!" she roared, and picked up a pipe. "Get out of here!"

Needles easily dodged the first swing that hit the cash register. Needles shoved her back against a bike rack, toppling her and the bikes.

He turned to see the old man holding a gun. He was steady as a rock, aiming the gun right at his forehead.

The doorbell rang and the man from the flower shop stepped in. "Artie, I heard — oh."

Needles knew he couldn't outrun a bullet. He stood his ground, watching the gun. Maybe he could get in and tackle the old man. Maybe he could throw the pump at him and distract him. Maybe ...

"Artie, put the gun down," said the man from the flower shop.

"I'm sick and tired of you people," Artie said. "I'm trying to run a business and you people are running me into the ground."

"Artie ..." the man from the flower shop walked slowly up to the counter. "This isn't the way —"

The woman in the coveralls jumped onto Needles' back. Needles turned around, presenting the woman's back to the gun, knowing the man wouldn't shoot his own daughter. At the same time, the man from the flower shop moved, somehow running between Needles and the woman, to get behind the counter. Needles had to deal with a woman punching him in the head while the other two men tussled. The gun went off.

Everything went quiet as the gunshot's echo ran through them all. The woman slipped off his back. The man from the flower shop stood holding the gun. Artie was shaken, but unharmed. The woman was also shaking.

"Now, can we talk like civilized people?" said the man from the flower shop, as he held the gun loosely. He set it down on the counter, out of Artie's reach, but well within Needles and his own. "How much do you owe?"

"Thirty dollars," said Artie.

The man from the flower shop nodded. "Come next door. I'll pay it."

"Don't pay it, Matt."

Matt walked behind the counter and touched Needles' arm. "Come with me."

Needles followed Matt next door. Matt flipped the sign to closed and locked the door.

"You're a new enforcer?" he asked as he walked to his cash register.

"I guess," Needles said. "I thought you were a Jew, what with the sign and all."

"Bought the place from one. Never changed the sign." He rang up the cash register and pulled out four ten-dollar bills.

"That should take care of him and me for this week."

Needles pocketed the money. He studied the man in profile, and something occurred to him. That's when the scent of roses and lavender washed over him, and he immediately got hard.

It was forbidden: the idea, the act. It was why he dreamed about it — the idea of feeling a man underneath him, giving way. He'd had a girl once, but it was quick, and it was a job to her. It was a job to all of the girls that he knew.

Matt was staring at him. "You, um, want anything else?"

He wanted the forbidden. He wanted to feel this man, like he had felt him in the dream.

Needles' body moved on its own volition. He stalked around the counter, and Matt backed into the corner, watching him. Needles' parted the curtain that separated the store from the back room. Matt stepped inside. Needles looked down at the man's ass in his pants, and he got so hard it hurt.

Needles dropped the curtain. Matt turned to him. The back room was full of ends of flowers in trash cans, half-made arrangements, flowers in water, and plants in pots. Needles noted the neatness of the place before he grabbed Matt's head with both of his large hands and held him while he kissed him.

Matt moaned, returned the kiss, like it happened in his dream. Matt's hands roamed underneath the suit jacket to the thin shirt beneath that already stretched tightly across his chest.

Needles set his hands on Matt's shoulders. He pushed him down, and Matt slowly dropped to his knees. Matt's hands moved down Needles' pants, and started unbuttoning the fly.

"Jesus," whispered Needles, as Matt inhaled his cock the minute it was free.

Matt bobbed his head. He was so much better than a woman, a larger mouth that could take him, and he wasn't afraid. Matt dove his head all the way down into Needles' pubes, and Needles looked down to watch.

Matt moaned and groaned, obviously enjoying himself as he licked and sucked and swallowed. Needles cast his head back, trying to hold himself back. He wanted this feeling to last longer. He clenched his hands into fists.

"Fuck, I swear ..."

Matt lifted his head, and stroked him instead. Needles missed the feeling of Matt's hot mouth, but knew what Matt was going for. That thought put Needles over the edge, and he exploded, all over Matt's smiling face.

Needles rocked, opening his fists. Matt sighed, and leaned back. He got up, his face still a mess, and walked over to his bench. He picked up a wet towel and wiped his face.

"That was good," Needles said, stuffing himself back into his pants, being sure not to drip on them.

"Thanks," said Matt, turning around and smiling.

Needles saw that Matt was tented in his pants, but he didn't make a move toward Needles. Needles didn't know what to do.

Matt looked around the room, slowly blushing. "Sorry about the mess back here."

"Don't worry. It smells good."

"So do you."

Matt came up to him. They both were about the same height but Needles was bigger than Matt. Matt placed a hand on Needles' chest.

Needles wanted to thrust his chest into Matt's hand, but he took a step back. "I gotta go."

Matt stepped back, thrust his hands in his pockets. "I understand."

The next words came out of his mouth before Needles could stop himself. "We can do it again sometime."

Matt smiled. "We can. I'll let you out."

Matt squeezed by Needles, pressing his back against Needles' chest. Needles put his hands on Matt's waist and guided him past. Matt thrust his ass against Needles' groin.

"Dammit," Needles whispered, as Matt chuckled.

He continued past Needles, unlocked the door, and let the big man out.

6

"What's this?"

Tony stared at the forty dollars that Needles threw down on the table.

"Don't bother the bike shop," Needles said. "The flower shop next door's picking up the tab."

"He paid you all this?"

"Yeah."

"He must be rich."

Needles shrugged. "Didn't seem like it to me."

"Find out."

"He bought the place from a Jew. He's not Jewish."

"When did he buy it?"

"How hell should I know?"

"You're gonna ask him. Find out how much he's worth and we'll push the price up."

Needles didn't like where this was going. "I don't think he's worth it."

"If the Mick can have a flower shop and makes a killing, then this guy must be doing the same."

Needles sighed. "I'll ask him tomorrow. I gotta get home."

"Give mama a kiss and find out when the hell Timothy will get his ass off the pot and come work for us."

He guessed his father might have something to do with that. That, and how Johnny ended up.

Needles walked home in the dark. Nobody bothered him in the neighborhood, which was good, because he didn't want to be bothered.

He stepped into the house, and his mother was already at the door, a wooden spoon in her hand and a stern look on her face.

"Where were you?"

"Had to do some work."

"Everyone asked about you. You're going to end up like Johnny."

"No, Mama. I don't pack heat."

"They don't care. They'll shoot you first."

"I don't do the kind of stuff Johnny did."

"Yet." If he had his way, he wouldn't do it.

Needles walked up to his mother and held his arms out. He smiled at her. "I won't do it. I promise."

She hmphed, turned to walk away, but Needles hugged her anyway.

"I'll be careful."

"That's what Johnny said." She pulled out of the hug and walked to the kitchen, leaving Needles standing alone.

7

Needles walked up to the flower shop and pulled on the handle of the door. It didn't budge. Then he saw the "Closed" sign on the door.

He peered through the window. He thought he could see someone moving in the back, but he wasn't sure. He felt stupid, leaning on the glass, trying to see in the dimly lit shop.

It took a while, but he finally saw Matt come out from behind the curtain. Needles tapped on the window, and Matt saw him at the window. He smiled, and came over to the door.

"What are you doing out here?" Matt asked.

"Need to talk to you."

"Come in. But I need to get some work done."

Needles stepped inside and Matt locked the door behind him.

Matt went over to the side of the wall and pulled out a bouquet of white roses. "My supplier is late. I have to take from the stock."

"Whatchu gotta do?"

"Wedding."

"Anyone I know?"

"Know any Polish people?"

"No." Needles chuckled.

"Then no one you know." Matt held open the curtain for Needles to step inside. "Why are you called Needles?"

He shrugged. "I useta be really skinny. My brother called me that, an' it just stuck."

Matt pulled out one of the roses and threaded it into a small wire basket. He wove the stem among the wires like his mother sewed.

"Did you like the flowers for your brother?" Matt asked.

"They were nice."

Matt snorted. "You didn't even notice."

"I noticed. The roses on the coffin were nice."

"It's called a blanket."

He wove another flower in the basket. He passed his hand over the bud, petting it gently. Needles could have sworn the scent of the rose got stronger.

Needles sniffed the air. "You do something to the flowers?"

He smiled as he wove the flowers. "Show them love and caring and they blossom."

Needles leaned against the other workbench that had four completed boutonnieres. "How come you make so much money?"

"How much money do you think I make?"

"You made enough to pay for that old man. And here." He watched Matt's back as he worked. "They might ask you for more."

"They, who?"

"The Outfit."

He turned around. "Everyone around here pays five dollars a week. It's what Irving told me when I bought the place."

"They might. If you make a lot of money."

Matt put his hands on his hips. "Are you here to tell me that my payments for protection are going to get increased?"

Needles scuffed the side of his shoe against the wooden floor and hunched his shoulders.

Matt said, "They're not going to get another dime out of me. Did they send you to make sure I paid more?"

"No. They want me ta find out what you make."

"It's none of their damn business what I make." He pointed at the back door, leading out into the rear alley. "I have to spend a hundred dollars a week just for stock! How much do you think I get when I do these weddings? Thirty ... forty dollars? Did you see what I charged for your brother's flowers? It's wholesale because I know they'll pay me whatever the hell they want to pay me! And I have to shut up and take it."

"Sure you ain't Jewish?"

"Very funny."

Needles smiled.

Matt turned to his flowers. "I can't afford the protection money I have. And I'm paying for Artie just to be a good neighbor. I don't want his place trashed, because it'll look bad for me."

Needles didn't quite understand what that meant, but Matt continued to weave flowers. He lifted the bouquet, woven with roses and greens. He put it among the boutonnieres.

"Six more to go."

"Flowers like that?"

"No, smaller ones. Carnations, thankfully."

He picked up three white carnations and braided their stems together, adding one or two greens for fullness. Needles watched him, mesmerized at how he wove them into a bouquet.

"How do you do that?"

"Many years of practice."

"Same thing when you give blow jobs?"

Matt turned to him. "That's because I enjoy it."

"You don't enjoy this?" Needles motioned to the flowers.

"I enjoy this immensely. But it's not the same as giving a blow job."

"What do you enjoy more?"

Carrying three completed bouquets, Matt walked over to Needles. He placed the flowers down, then brushed his hand across Needles' crotch.

"Depends."

Needles looked down. His pants stretched across his hardening member.

"On what?"

"Whether the other party wants to try something different."

"Different how?"

"Ever fuck a man?"

Needles stiffened, both in fright and anticipation. "No, never did."

"Ever want to?" Matt traced a finger down Needles' button-down shirt, flicking at the buttons, teasing to unbutton them.

"Thought about it," Needles said, thinking back to his dream.

Matt pulled his hand away. "Let me go lock the door."

Needles parted the curtain and Matt walked by him. Needles watched the tight ass in the dungarees, and wondered whether it was just as tight beneath them. Matt turned the lock, and the plants in the place seemed to shudder, leaves rustled.

Matt returned, taking off the blue apron. Underneath he only wore a t-shirt, since it was hot in the back here. Needles watched, but didn't help, him take off the shirt.

He was more muscular than Needles expected. Needles reached out and touched the bare, nearly hairless skin of the man.

"Take off your shirt," Matt said, "Or let me take it off for you."

"Go ahead," said Needles.

Matt grinned and deftly undid the buttons, including the ones on his pants. Matt parted the shirt, sighed, and buried his face into Needles' chest.

Needles gasped. He reached down and shoved down Matt's dungarees, while Matt sucked on a nipple.

Needles moaned, shoving down his own pants next, and he couldn't help but grab his own cock. Matt slapped his hand away and grabbed Needles' cock instead, stroking it slowly.

Needles then reached down and grabbed Matt's tight ass. It was firm, strong, as he squeezed it. Matt drove his cock against Needles' and both men groaned loudly.

"Fuck me now," Matt said, turning around.

He took out a jar, and smeared what was inside onto Needles' cock.

"Oil," he said. "Smoother."

"Turn around," growled Needles.

Matt turned around and offered his ass to him. Needles poked, unsure of where the place was. Then he found it, because Matt moved in just the right place. Needles drove it inside, while Matt screamed.

It was so tight, he almost came right there. But he slowed down, and rocked his body back and forth, forcing himself to hold on, to feel the rise of the orgasm, listening to Matt under him grunt and groan in pure pleasure.

This was better than the bitch he'd fucked.

"Now," Matt cried out, and he threw his head back, his body stiffening for a moment.

He cried out, and the tightness got even more tight around Needles' unbelievably hard cock. Needles lost it.

Driving deep within him, Needles exploded inside Matt, holding Matt's body close to him. He fell forward, onto the table in front of them, crushing Matt between his body and the table.

"Shit," was all Needles could say.

8

After that, Needles didn't avoid the flower shop, but he had to do other things. Since he had done such a good job at collecting money the first time, they sent him to different stores to collect more money. The Outfit trusted him to return with the correct amount of money he was sent to collect, as opposed to some other guys who would pocket a couple of dollars here and there.

He found himself spending more and more time with Tony, as well. Tony seemed to be grooming Needles for something, but he wasn't sure what. Needles knew that you didn't screw with the Outfit's women or their money, so he kept his nose clean that way.

His mother's birthday was coming up. He decided to get her something special. He had saved up enough money for a mother-of-pearl ring. He had the money on him as he walked to the jeweller across the street from Matt's shop.

He planned on buying the ring, then stopping at Matt's to pick up a bouquet of roses.

As he approached the jeweller's, he saw two cops coming toward him. He didn't know them, but his heart skipped a beat. Most of the cops were on the take, at least as far as he knew, but these guys were giving him the once-over as they approached.

Needles had nowhere to run, even if he did. He kept walking, avoiding looking at them.

"Hey," one man called.

Needles turned.

"What's in your pocket?"

Needles had his hand in his pocket, mostly to protect the wad of cash he had for the ring. He pulled his hand out, empty. If they knew he had cash, they might take it from him.

They grabbed him and put him against the wall, frisking him. One man put his hand in his pocket and came out with the money. "What's a guy like you doing with all this money?"

"I'm buyin' a ring for my mother."

The cop flicked through the money with his thumb. "Lots of money here for a ring."

Needles didn't say anything as the cop pocketed the money. Then they let him go.

"Consider it a toll, Wop."

The cops walked away, laughing. Needles stood there, seething. Now he had nothing to give his mother.

He looked across the street. Maybe Matt could give him something on credit. He hated the idea of asking, but he couldn't return home with nothing. He hunched his shoulders and went across the street to the flower shop.

Matt was sitting behind the counter, listening to the radio when Needles walked in.

"Needles!" he said, getting to his feet. "It's been a while."

"Been busy."

"I know. Someone not quite as handsome as you has been collecting from me these past couple of weeks. What's wrong?"

"Fuckin' cops took my money. I was gonna get somethin' for Mama's birthday." He looked directly at Matt. "I hate t' ask—"

"I'll give you a bouquet for your mother."

"I'll pay you next week—"

"Nonsense." Matt got up and went to his stock. "How old is she?"

"Dunno. Forty?"

Matt laughed. "Two dozen roses are enough, then it gets ostentatious."

"Osten ...?"

"Overwhelming. Too fancy. Like you're trying too hard."

Matt did some quick weaving, found a fancy crystal vase, and put the flowers into it.

"Give them a little water every day, they'll last for a month."

Needles took the bouquet from him. "Thanks. I really mean it."

Matt only smiled. "Go home and give that to your Mama. Give her a kiss from me."

Needles laughed and left the flower shop.

He went home, and his mother squealed with delight at the flowers and the crystal vase. She buried her face in the roses and inhaled their scent. He hadn't seen her so happy since before his brother died.

She placed the flowers on the kitchen table and admired them. "They're beautiful."

His father walked in, smelling of garbage. The scent of roses filled the room, as if trying to overpower the odor of his father. The roses won as his father walked through the kitchen to the bathroom. His mother got up to boil water for his bath.

Timothy didn't come home for dinner. His father had to ask what the flowers were for. After dinner, he left the apartment to go to the bar.

Needles waited up with his mother until Timothy came home, which was after his father crawled in from the bar. Timothy didn't even kiss his mother hello, but slunk into the bedroom. Needles got up and followed him.

"Where the hell you been?"

"None o' your business."

Needles sniffed the air. "You been drinkin'."

"Yeah. Why can't I drink?"

"You know what it does to dad … what it did to Johnny."

Timothy shoved Needles. "To hell with you."

Needles shoved him back. Timothy raised a hand and Needles grabbed Timothy's wrist.

"What the hell is wrong with you?"

Timothy pulled his hand out of Needles' grip. "Fuck you. At least I'm not a momma's boy."

"It's her birthday today."

"So what?"

Needles slapped Timothy so hard that he fell backwards into the bed.

"Stop fighting!" their mother yelled from the doorway.

Timothy scrambled to sit up, his fist against the corner of his bleeding mouth. He glared at Needles, who glared back, with his hands clenched at his sides.

"I'm leaving," Timothy said, and walked out of the room, shoving past Needles, while his mother stepped aside.

His father didn't dare come out. His mother sat down at the dark kitchen table and cried.

The scent of roses filled the room.

9

Needles marched into his Uncle Tony's office at the garage. Tony looked up and then to the side. Two men from the Outfit stood there, trying to look casual, but definitely packing heat.

"Whatsematter?" Tony asked.

"What're you doing with Timothy?"

"Timothy who?"

"My brother, Timothy."

"Not doin' anything. Your Mama's lost too much already."

Needles looked at the two impassive statues standing next to the desk. They gazed on him like they could take him out back and beat the crap out of him with one look from Tony. Needles didn't want to give them that chance.

"Why, whatsematter?"

Tony didn't know. Maybe Timothy was running with someone outside of the Outfit. Maybe he had a girlfriend. In a bar. Sure, that could be it.

"Nuthin'," Needles said. He hunched his shoulders. "Sorry, I thought —"

"You ain't paid to think," said Tony with a grin. He scribbled out something on a piece of paper. "Go pick up some money from this street. Everybody owes."

Needles took the paper and glanced at it. It was a street that had been Mick territory, but he guessed there must have been a fight to gain it.

"Can you do it by yourself?" asked Tony.

"Yeah, sure." He crumpled the piece of paper in his pocket.

"You might want a piece."

"I don't need a gun."

Since Johnny had gotten killed with one in his hand, he didn't want to get caught with one. People would get the wrong idea — that he was a thug. He was better than that, he thought.

Soon enough, Needles had a beat — four blocks of businesses and houses — where he would collect the protection money and bring it to his Uncle Tony. He never skimmed or shook people down for more protection money so that he could line his own pockets.

Matt was one of his "customers", and he would go in almost daily to visit him. Sometimes they would just talk. Other times, Matt would put the "Closed" sign on the door and the two men would have a couple of hours with each other in the back room. Always among the flowers, smelling sweetly throughout the room, Needles would take Matt mercilessly.

One hot afternoon, the two men sat across from each other in the back room. Needles had gone through his "customers" for the week, and now was thinking about how to get Matt out of his clothes. Matt was already in a tank shirt, the apron over it, looking sexy enough for Needles.

Then, the door opened in the front. Matt got up, caressed Needles' jaw, and said, "Be right back."

He stepped out to the front, and Needles could hear him say, "Can I help you?"

"You Matt Perrault?"

"Yes." Then a few seconds later, Needles heard Matt yell, "Hey!"

Needles got up, noting the tone was of shock. He next heard a shot, and Needles threw back the curtain to the back room.

One of the men from Uncle Tony's garage stood in the doorway at the front door, a gun in his hand. Then, suddenly, a vine came from his left side and whipped around the man's wrist. Another vine twisted around the man's feet. Another vine from the ceiling dropped down and wrapped around the man's neck.

The man tried to bat away the vines, but they had thorns, scraping and scratching him. He dropped the pistol. The vine from the ceiling tightened around the man's neck, pulling him up off the ground.

"What the hell?"

Needles stared at Matt, who glared at the man as the vines pulled him up by his neck. Vines wrapped around the man's torso, pulling his arms to his sides. He struggled as the vines choked him.

"He came to hurt me," Matt said, coldly and calmly, as the man twisted in the doorway.

"I know him," Needles said. "He's with the Outfit."

"I don't care where he's from," Matt said. "Nobody comes into my home to hurt me."

Needles wasn't sure what to do. Should he try to save the guy? Or was Matt right?

The man slowly strangled in the doorway. The vines seemed to know when the man was dead, because they dropped him onto the floor of the flower shop, right in front of the doorway.

Matt walked up to the man and picked up the pistol he had dropped. He gently toed the man in the side, but the man didn't move.

"They're gonna come after you, Matt."

"Why did they come after me now?" He looked at Needles. "Who sent him? Why?"

"I dunno."

Would his Uncle Tony have sent him? But Matt was paying his dues right along.

"Help me get this body out of here."

"Where?"

"Downstairs in the cellar."

Needles bent down and dragged the body out of the way of the swinging door, while Matt shut the door and put the "Closed" sign up. Hoisting the heavy body over his shoulder, stumbling because of the weight, Needles followed Matt into the back room. Matt moved one of the work tables. In the floor was a trap door.

Matt pulled up on the trap door and the entire door came out. It was only five by five, barely enough room for Needles to get in. A set of rickety wooden stairs led into a thick gloom.

A light flashed on, a lantern on a stick. There was nothing down here but a dirt floor. The lantern lit a small patch of dirt to the right of the rickety stairs.

"Right here," said Matt, pointing to the ground.

Panting, Needles dropped the man onto the dirt. Dust kicked up when he did, and he coughed.

"We need a shovel and —"

"No need," said Matt, as he bent and touched the ground.

Needles watched as the ground opened up: first a crack, then a hole, and the man sank into the hole, leaving a mound of dirt above. He watched as that, too, leveled off.

The vines, the dirt, the flowers—the pieces fell into place. Needles stared at Matt, who looked back at him. He bowed his head and went to the lantern, snuffing out the light. The only light now came from upstairs. Needles scrambled up the stairs, wanting to get away from Matt.

Needles debated whether or not to just leave. Something wasn't right with Matt. But he wanted Matt to explain it. And there was no way he was going to his Uncle Tony to say he was an accomplice to a murder.

Matt came up the stairs. "I'm sorry you had to see that."

"What the hell are you?"

Matt winced. "I'm just like you. A little different."

"A little? You did that, didn't you? You made the ground open up."

"Yes."

"And the vines. You did that."

"Some of it ..."

"The flowers. You make them grow."

"I give them a longer life."

"How?"

Matt turned to the trap door. "You'd better sit down."

"I'll stand."

Matt fitted the trap door back into place, then moved the workbench over it. He sat down on the stool next to the table.

"I am a soldier of Ishtar."

"Where's that?"

"Who's that, really. She's a goddess of Mesopotamia. The Middle East?" At the lack of recognition, he said, "Persia?"

"Oh, yeah, Persia."

"I was selected by Ishtar to assist people when they need it." He motioned to the flowers on the bench. "In return, she gave me the power over plants and the earth."

"Are you kidding?"

"No, I'm not kidding." He looked away. "Now that you know, I have to leave town."

"What? Why?"

"People talk."

Needles walked over to him. "I ain't gonna talk."

Matt still wouldn't look at Needles. "I just killed one of your friends."

"He wasn't my friend." He took Matt's chin and pulled his head up, looking into Matt's eyes. "You're my friend."

Matt closed his eyes and made a soft noise in his throat.

"If you leave, I'm comin' with you."

"You would?" Matt said quietly, opening his eyes.

"Yeah. Yeah, I would."

He'd leave Mama and Timothy to their own devices, and he would leave town with Matt. They could probably go somewhere farther West, maybe even California.

Matt kissed Needles, and the two fell into an embrace. Needles wasn't sure if the man he hugged was human or not, but he sure felt like it.

YOU MIGHT ALSO ENJOY

Cancer
A Brothers of the Zodiac Story
by Maxwell Thomas

Two outcasts in 1930's Kansas City meet and one becomes the man he's meant to be.

Pisces
A Brothers of the Zodiac Story
by Maxwell Thomas

A young doctor in Union-occupied New Orleans questions his passion for a dashing Union sergeant.

Scorpio
A Brothers of the Zodiac Story
by Maxwell Thomas

A young man goes to a gay bar in St. Louis, and finds himself an angel who turns out to be a breaker of taboos.

Available from Zarra Knightley Publishing
in trade paperback, digital, and audio editions.

zarraknightleypublishing.com

www.ingramcontent.com/pod-product-compliance
Lightning Source LLC
Chambersburg PA
CBHW022040170626
46808CB00003B/1288